A Very Marcello

Christmas

BETHANY-KRIS

Published by Bethany-Kris

www.bethanykris.com

eISBN 13: 978-1-988197-47-0

Print ISBN 13: 978-1-988197-48-7

Cover Art © Sasha Elle

Editor: Elizabeth Peters

Contents

Chapter One...5

Chapter Two... 11

Chapter Three... 18

Chapter Four.. 26

Chapter Five... 35

Chapter Six... 42

Chapter Seven... 49

Chapter Eight 56

Chapter Nine.. 63

Chapter Ten.. 70

Chapter Eleven 77

Chapter Twelve.. 87

Chapter Thirteen....................................... 95

Chapter Fourteen.....................................102

Chapter Fifteen 110

Chapter Sixteen..117

Chapter Seventeen 124

Chapter Eighteen 131

Chapter Nineteen.....................................139

CHAPTER TWENTY 147
CHAPTER TWENTY-ONE 155
CHAPTER TWENTY-TWO 162
CHAPTER TWENTY-THREE 169
CHAPTER TWENTY-FOUR 177
CHAPTER TWENTY-FIVE 185
CHAPTER TWENTY-SIX 192

Antony & Cecelia

December 1st

Calendars were things made by the Devil, surely. Each time Cecelia Marcello looked at one, she was reminded of something else she had forgotten to do. Or a birthday coming up. Someone's school event. Holidays.

Too many things, too little hours, she thought.

It was always something.

Really, she wasn't too surprised. It was expected with a family like the Marcellos. A family as large as theirs was always navigating tasks, important happenings, and all the while, trying not to step on someone else's toes.

Her three sons, their wives, and their children

certainly made for interesting weeks.

Lucian, their oldest through adoption, and his wife Jordyn had three children. Two girls, and a boy. A very *wild* boy. Cecelia thought her oldest and his wife were finally done having children, as they assured that was the case, but she didn't know for sure. Anything was possible, and she was hoping for at least one more grandchild.

Dante, their oldest biological son, and his wife, Catrina, had two children. One girl that was far too much like her mother, and an older boy that was far too smart for his own good. Those two siblings fought like cats and dogs, but Cecelia usually found herself amused by the two more so than annoyed.

And finally, Giovanni. Their youngest, and the *most* rebellious of their children. He and his wife, Kim, had given them only one grandchild. Little Andino. At six, almost seven, Andino was not the handful his other cousins could be. He was a quiet boy, always looking out for others, and sweet as could be. Cecelia, at first, had been sad that Giovanni and Kim chose not to have more children after Andino, but now …

Well, she supposed if they were only going to have one, a perfect *principe* was just as wonderful.

"December seventeenth," Jordyn said over the phone. "That's for John's Christmas concert."

"And Liliana's kindergarten Christmas concert?"

"Same day—in the morning. Supposed to start at ten."

Cecelia frowned. "I suppose we're lucky that Michel is in the same school as John. That saves a date."

"Not Andino, though," Jordyn pointed out.

No, because Giovanni refused to put his son in private schools. It wasn't the cost, but rather, her son wanted Andino to be around all kinds of people. Not only spoiled, rich, white people. Cecelia had once pointed out that Giovanni had gone to expensive, private establishments, but all she got was a dead stare in response.

Sometimes there were things better left unsaid.

This was one of those.

"Andino's Christmas concert is on the sixteenth," Cecelia said, tapping the date on the calendar with the tip of a sharpie marker. "Thankfully, it all works out."

Jordyn laughed. "Yeah, *this* year, Cecelia."

"Mmm, I know."

"Next year, Catherine will start school. The year after that, Cella. Someday, things are not going to coincide so well with your plans. Someone will have to deal with not seeing their grandmamma and grandpapa there. You know that's okay, right? We *understand*."

7

Perhaps, but Cecelia didn't.

"It is okay if you miss an event or two," Jordyn said again.

"Not if I can help it," Cecelia replied.

Jordyn sighed. "I'm just saying."

"How are you doing, darling?"

"I'm okay."

"Really?"

"Well …"

Cecelia turned away from the calendar to lean against the island counter. "Missing Lucian?"

"It's a very big house to be in when you're here alone."

"I bet."

"Ninety-eight more days," Jordyn said quietly.

"Maybe less, with good behavior."

Jordyn laughed. "He's a well-known *Mafioso* in jail on an illegal weapons charge. His last name alone is what's going to keep him in for the full sentence."

Already, Lucian had been in for a couple of months. It would be another three before he was home with his wife and children. It broke Cecelia's heart because he was so adored by his family, and missed. The law did not care, though.

"He'll be home soon," Cecelia said.

"I know." Jordyn cleared her throat. "Well, I just called to let you know the final, for-sure dates of the kids' concerts. I was thinking of stopping by tomorrow, too, if you didn't mind."

"Of course, I don't mind. You could also drop off John, Liliana, and Cella, if you wanted. Take a night for yourself—a break. We all need them. You more so than others, right now."

"Well …"

"Jordyn, drop them off and give yourself a break. Okay?"

Finally, her daughter-in-law said, "Okay, Cecelia. Thank you."

Soon after, Cecelia hung up the phone. Once more, she turned to the calendar on the wall, and felt like the damn thing was haunting her. Between all the grandchildren's events coming up, a visit to see Lucian in jail, a charity auction she had agreed to help put on, and all the church functions … it was going to be a *very* busy Christmas.

That wasn't even starting on the New Year.

Still, there was only one thing Cecelia could think that she wanted. As usual, her husband would do something amazing. He would give her something spectacular. Antony never failed in that regard, even when she told him year after year that he didn't need to do that sort of thing.

Yet, she wished for her family. All of them, for at least one single day, to be in the same house together. It was getting harder and harder to do as the kids became older, and focuses changed. Just once more … she wanted them all together.

Or at the very least, *happy*.

Surely, that wasn't too much to ask.

Heading to the table, Cecelia grabbed the rolls of wrapping paper that she had forgotten on the floor when the phone started to ring. For now, she would settle herself on wrapping presents, and finish decorating the main rooms of the mansion.

That in itself was a job meant for an army.

It was only December first, after all.

They had time to figure out the rest.

Chapter 2

December 5th

"Isn't it beautiful?" Cecelia asked.

Her husband tugged her closer into his side as they walked through the park. "Very, *Tesoro.*"

"I like that they went with red and white this year."

"It's quite striking against the backdrop, isn't it?" Cecelia agreed.

The park had been decorated with giant red and white boughs of holly between thick ropes of fir garland. A few of the choke cherry trees kept their red bulbs, and while snow covered the branches, the color still peeked through. Multicolored lights lit up the trees as they continued their stroll through the quiet park.

Heavy snowflakes fell from the sky.

Already, they had a few inches of snow on the ground. It wasn't much, and usually, it would be gone within the hour it fell thanks to New York weather. They typically didn't get snow that stuck until later in the month, closer to Christmas.

This year was a different story.

Cecelia considered it an early Christmas gift.

"I see you added new dates to the calendar this morning," Antony noted.

"Christmas concerts."

"We'll be running for days."

She smiled. "Would you have it any other way?"

Antony chuckled, drew her closer into his warm embrace, and kissed the wool hat covering her temple. "Never, *amore*."

Their walk was mostly silent, as it usually was when they got the chance to take five minutes out of their busy days to be together. Despite their constant movement, her husband always made time to remind Cecelia how much he loved her, and how much their life meant to him. She appreciated it more than she could explain.

Especially during the holidays.

Their life was not always perfect. Over the years, they

had more than their fair share of sad moments and hard times. Struggles that shaped their marriage, and family, into the pillars of faith, strength, and love it now was.

Cecelia wouldn't dare ask for a single thing to be done differently.

Time had treated them especially well.

"You know," she said, peering up at her dark-haired, green-eyed love, "this is still my favorite time of the year."

"I know," Antony replied.

His arm tightened around her, and his light laughter came with a white puff of air from his lips. It was just cold enough to see their breaths, but not enough to be uncomfortable.

"How do you know?"

"Well, for one, because it gives you a reason to shop."

"Don't you say that, Antony!"

"It's true."

Cecelia guffawed, and smacked her husband with the back of her hand. An *oof* sound fell from his smirking mouth before he grabbed her mitten-covered hand and snuck it inside his jacket. The tautness of his stomach pressed against her mitten, and the warmth of his body bled into hers.

"It is not," she said with a pout.

"Kind of is."

"Antony."

"Cecelia, you shop for everyone," he muttered, "even the girl at the grocery store who bags your groceries. You even buy Giovanni's ugly dog treats to last him the whole year."

"Well ... he's a good dog!"

Antony glanced away, but not before Cecelia saw the roll of his eyes. "Barely good."

"You're ruining my Christmas spirit."

"Nothing can ruin your Christmas spirt, Cecelia. You're the angel on top of the tree. You're the star that hangs high in the sky, calling all your family home to celebrate. You are the—"

"Okay, I get it," she whispered with a smile. "Thank you."

Antony stopped their walk, turning to hold Cecelia in his embrace, and stare down at her. Familiar, yet haunting eyes, watched her in that way of his. He could silence her with a look, love her with a linger, and tease her with a wink. That had never once changed in all their many years of marriage.

Neither had the way he adored and loved her.

Familiarity was their best friend.

"Why is it still your favorite time of year, *Tesoro*?"

Cecelia cupped his face. Her fingers were toasty warm

under the thick mittens. "Because you have given me decades and decades of happy Christmases, Antony. Memories after memories that I can never forget. Sure, some things have changed over the years. Our children are all grown up with babies of their own. We're a little older than we once were, but it's still just as wonderful and beautiful."

Antony grinned. "Old, huh?"

"Was that seriously all you heard in that?"

"You know how I feel when you call me old, Cecelia."

She huffed out a laugh, and stood on her tiptoes in her leather boots to kiss his mouth. "Don't worry, Antony. I'm very aware that age has not caught up with you quite yet. You remind me as much as you possibly can."

Even at their ages, passion was still *very* much alive.

Cecelia was also quite grateful for that.

Antony's grin turned sinful. "I do, don't I?"

"That's quite enough. I'm not feeding your ego today."

"No, we'll save that for later."

"*Dio,*" Cecelia mumbled, half in curse, half in prayer. She wasn't quite sure how she was going to keep up with this man for the rest of her life, but damn her if she wasn't going to at least *try*. Didn't she owe him that, after everything? "Should we get back home and finish decorating?"

Antony made a face. "In a moment. I never asked, but what did you want for Christmas this year?"

Cecelia lifted a single brow high. "Why, haven't you already gotten it for me?"

"Perhaps I have *something*."

"But?"

"But you may want something else, too."

She did.

She absolutely did want something else.

"I'm not sure you could give me what I'm wishing for," Cecelia admitted, "and it would not be because you are incapable of being amazing, Antony."

He frowned. "I don't understand."

"I was thinking this might be one of the last years we could have everyone together for Christmas morning. Together, and happy. Considering how old the kids are getting, their interests and activities are picking up … Someday, we're going to start losing people from the big table."

"I see what you mean."

"Also," Cecelia added, "Lucian is in jail."

"He's doing fine. He'll be out in three months."

"No, I know. I just meant … my wish is impossible

16

with him being where he is, that's all."

Antony nodded. "Well, how about something different?"

"Like what?"

"What if I gave everyone else exactly what they wanted? What if I made them the happiest they could be this year? Would that suit your needs? Next year, I will make sure to get them all together on Christmas morning, no matter what. This year, let me make them happy."

"Are you going to play Santa?"

Antony flashed his teeth in a smile, and winked. "Ho, ho, ho, Cecelia."

December 7th

"Do you think I should throw our annual Christmas party this year?" Cecelia asked.

Antony peered over the edge of the *Car and Driver* magazine he had been perusing for close to an hour as Cecelia readied for bed. "Bit late to start considering a party that large, isn't it?"

"Well, I know I usually begin planning earlier."

"Yes, at the start of November, Cecelia."

She met his gaze in the vanity mirror while she massaged lotion into her hands. "What if I handed the reins over this year?"

"To who?"

"The girls."

Antony lifted a single brow. "The boys' wives, you mean."

"Who else would I be talking about, Antony?"

"Hard to say with you," he mumbled under his breath.

Cecelia shot him a look, but Antony only winked in response.

"Would you actually *do* that, though?" he asked.

"Do what?"

"Hand the reins over, as you said. Give up control. Don't micromanage every detail over their shoulders. Let them have the freedom to actually plan."

"You make me sound like a tyrant."

"You are," he replied easily, "especially when it comes to parties or your kitchen."

"I am—"

Antony's green gaze pinned Cecelia in place as he said, "You absolutely are. I didn't say it was a bad thing, *Tesoro*, but own it, at the very least."

She sighed dramatically. "They don't complain."

"No, because they love you."

"I think you're exaggerat—"

"Cecelia, you broke my knuckle with a wooden spoon

once when I meddled with a *stew*."

"I apologized for that!"

"And yet, here I am, still bringing it up."

"*Antony*."

He chuckled from his side of the bed. "I'm kidding, *amore*."

Cecelia pouted. "I don't think you are."

"Half-kidding, then."

She loved her husband.

Even when he infuriated her.

"I would," she insisted.

"Would what?"

"Hand over the reins to the girls."

Antony stared up at the ceiling. "If you want to have a party that badly, then we'll have one. No need to try to convince me with lies about letting the girls plan it."

"It's not lies."

"Cecelia."

"I'm Catholic. I don't know how to lie." *Sort of*, she added silently. "The nuns beat that out of you in Catholic schools."

"The nuns were the worst."

"See, you agree. Now about this party …"

Antony chuckled under his breath, and shook his head. "Okay, then let the girls plan, but I mean actually let them *plan*, Cecelia. No stepping in. No making demands. No traditional if they want modern. No ordering them to cook every last dish when it's already this late in the month, and it would just be easier to get a caterer."

"Oh, my God, a *caterer*?"

"And there's your *no*," Antony said.

Cecelia pressed her lips together tightly before forcing herself to say, "Okay, a *caterer*."

"Stop saying it like that."

"Like what, Antony?"

"Like it makes you want to scream."

"But it does!"

"Maybe they will cook. I didn't say they wouldn't. I said you needed to let them decide, *should* they agree to plan it."

This was going to be harder than Cecelia first thought.

"I know the girls can throw a good party," she said after a long moment.

Antony smiled. "Then allow them to do that."

"*Fine.*"

"And stop making it sound like you're about to walk through hell for some eggnog."

Cecelia stood from the seat at her vanity, and turned to her husband. "You could … indulge me, Antony. Let me meddle a little."

"No."

"Antony."

"No."

"But—"

"*No.*"

"You are impossible!"

"Says you," Antony shot back. "Now get in bed, *donna.*"

Cecelia slipped under the covers just as Antony turned to shove the magazine into his nightstand. She expected him to roll back over empty-handed. Instead, he held a bright red folder. Wordlessly, he held it out for her to take.

She hesitated.

"What is it?"

"Something special," he told her.

"A gift?"

"A big gift."

"For …?"

"Christmas," Antony said, grinning, "now open it."

Cecelia plucked the folder from his hands with her own smile. "You couldn't wait for Christmas?"

"That would defeat the purpose."

"Of what?"

"Well, *open it*."

Cecelia enjoyed teasing her husband when she actually got the chance to, and that wasn't very often. Usually, it was him pulling tricks on her. She set the folder on top of the covers over her legs, and drummed her fingernails to the bright red top.

"You didn't spend very much time wrapping it, huh?"

"Cecelia."

"What?"

"Open that damn folder," Antony muttered.

"Gosh, you're so impatient."

"Someone's certainly *testing* my patience tonight."

She smiled sweetly. "Yes, but you like it."

"Would you open that folder?"

Deciding she had teased Antony enough, she quickly flipped open the top of the folder, and peered at the contents inside. Papers, it seemed. Documents of some kind. Cecelia picked up what looked to be a deed, and a small geo-map right underneath.

"What is this for?" she asked.

"Read it."

She did.

"An island?"

"A *private* island," Antony said.

"In the Caribbean."

"Yep."

There were a couple of photographs, too. A quaint, tri-level cottage with huge windows covering the front wall and a massive wrap-around porch sat in the middle of the island. It seemed the place was fitted with generators to maintain its own power supply, and boats to travel back and forth to the mainland. It was *beautiful*.

"Did you seriously buy me an island?"

"Depends on how you feel about it," Antony replied.

"Well …"

"Oh, and you need a way to get there, right?"

Cecelia glanced over at him.

Antony simply handed over a set of keys.

"What is this for?"

"A sixty-foot luxury yacht I decided to call *Beauty*."

"Antony …"

"Too much?" he asked.

"Yes," she said, "but not for you."

Without warning, Cecelia found herself pulled into her husband's lap. He kissed her mouth once, then twice, and grinned against her lips.

"So, *this* was probably why you didn't want me focusing on getting everybody together, right?"

Antony shrugged. "I would really like to try that island out."

Cecelia held his gaze as she stretched over his form.

"You better play one hell of a Santa, Antony Marcello."

"Already working on it, *Tesoro*."

She had no doubt.

Chapter 4

Lucian & Jordyn

December 5th

"John," Jordyn said, hitting her oldest child's door with a closed fist, "it's time to get up for school, come on."

Only grumbles answered her back. She checked the doorknob, but already knew what she would find. It was locked, effectively keeping her out.

"Christ, Lucian, you just had to give him a damn lock."

As soon as the words were out of her mouth, Jordyn regretted them. Mostly, because her husband wasn't actually there for her to say them to. Lucian was still serving out his sentence, with another three months to go.

God, she missed him.

Every day.

Every night.

First thing on her mind in the morning, and the last at night.

Next to their three kids, of course.

Speaking of kids …

"John, get up!"

Jordyn banged a little harder.

Still, she didn't hear the telltale sounds of her son. If at his age, John was already giving his parents hell, she could only imagine what it was going to be like in a few short years when he was a teenager. Her son was all kinds of difficult.

God save their souls.

She loved John.

Adored him.

She could still admit that out of their kids, he was the most difficult.

Putting it mildly.

The phone started ringing, making Jordyn cuss under her breath. They were already running late for school as it was, and she had two other kids to get out of bed and dressed. Liliana for kindergarten, and Cella, for pre-school.

This was not going well.

"John, two minutes and you better be up!"

That was the last warning she was giving her son before she broke his damn door down. Momma didn't play. Not when Dad wasn't around to help her keep their son in line.

The girls on the other hand?

They were far easier.

Jordyn darted down the hall to the master bedroom in order to catch the ringing phone before it sent the call to voicemail. There were very few people who would call their home this early, and the ones that would, she would answer. Their calls were important.

Family was always important. All her years with the Marcellos—*as* a Marcello—had taught her that lesson.

"Cella, Liliana, time to get up!" Jordyn shouted as she passed their rooms. "Right now, girls, up!"

She didn't wait to hear if her girls answered her back. Sliding into the master bedroom, Jordyn snatched the cordless phone off the hook on the fourth ring, thankfully.

"Hello?" she asked, out of breath.

"Hey, *bella.*"

Instantly, all the worries Jordyn felt slipped out the window just like that. She no longer cared that she was thirty minutes behind. She didn't mind that her son was being extra difficult likely because he missed his father. She didn't give a shit that she needed to clean the bathrooms, change everybody's sheets, and make it into the art gallery to set up for a showing.

Not one single bit of that mattered.

Not when she heard Lucian's voice.

"How's your morning going?" her husband asked.

"Better now."

"Oh?"

"It's always better when you call, Lucian."

She could hear his smile when he murmured, "Same, *amore*."

"You got your call earlier today, huh?"

"Figured I might as well take it. I didn't enjoy talking to the voicemail yesterday. It's not as good as talking to you."

"Agreed," Jordyn said, sitting down on the edge of their bed. "Something came up at Cella's pre-school. She swallowed her drink down the wrong hole, coughed her guts out, and then puked all over the place."

"She's not actually sick, though, right?"

"No, it's just their stupid policies. The second a kid gets sick, they send them home. I ran out to pick her up when you called. Sorry, Lucian."

"It's all right. She up right now?"

Jordyn listened for their daughters. The tiny pattering of feet in the hallway said that yes, they were awake and moving around, but not yet ready to make their way into their parents' bedroom.

"Just got up," she said. "Just a sec, Lucian."

Pulling the phone away, she put her hand over the receiver and shouted for the girls to come see her when they were done.

"Kay, Ma!" Liliana called back.

Jordyn fell back on their bed as she put the phone to her ear once more. She hated how cold and empty it was without him. She couldn't wait until he was back home with her and their children. Stupid circumstances and charges that he couldn't escape took him away from them. It killed her, but she said nothing. She didn't blame Lucian, though she probably could. He would likely take it, too.

Truth was, Jordyn understood their life. She knew exactly what she signed up for when she married her husband. Their life and freedom was not guaranteed. Her husband, his brothers, and the rest of their family were all criminals. Sometimes, jail and prison were likely scenarios. Her fear walked hand in hand with her respect.

It was what it was.

She would not fault Lucian for choices she made.

And she loved him.

Oh, she loved him.

"How's my boy doing this week?" Lucian asked.

Jordyn scoffed under her breath. "Same."

That was a lie.

John was worse than last week.

She didn't want Lucian to worry.

"He up?"

"In the shower," she lied.

He had far better things to mull over while in jail other than their son's concerning behavior. They would deal with it *together* when Lucian was out.

"Here come the girls," Jordyn said as a stampede of footsteps echoed down the hall.

Jordyn barely got the words out of her mouth before the girls barreled into the bedroom. They saw their mother on the phone, she hit the speaker button, and their squeals lit up the whole place.

Especially when Lucian said, "*Mia principessas!*"

"Daddy!"

"Dad-day!"

Liliana and Cella clambered onto the bed. The eldest snatched the phone from her mother, while the youngest crawled up Jordyn's back.

"Hi, Daddy," Liliana said. "Santa's coming in twenty

days!"

"Is he?" Lucian asked.

"Santa!" their three-year-old mocked.

"I wrote my letter to him yesterday at school," Liliana said seriously.

"What did you ask for, *ragazza?*"

Liliana started listing off the lengthy list that she had brought home to Jordyn the day before covered in markers, sparkles, and Santa stickers. A dollhouse. Those ugly, big-headed dolls with the crazy hair. Some kind of animal that came out of an egg. Clothes. *Shoes.*

And then, "And you, Daddy."

Jordyn stilled as her gaze darted to her eldest daughter. Lucian quieted on the phone.

"Santa will bring you home, won't he?" Liliana asked.

Lucian blew out a soft breath. "I don't know, Lily. We're … I'm awfully far away, sweetheart, and Santa has so many other kids to deliver presents to. Plus, we're very lucky, remember? Not like some other people, who are not as lucky, and don't get as many presents as you do. So, maybe this year, we'll go easy on Santa and not expect as much. So, then he has more time for those who are not as lucky."

Liliana frowned, and Jordyn swore she saw tears well in her daughter's eyes, but softly, she said, "Okay, Daddy."

"Dad-day!" Cella mocked.

Lucian chuckled. "Okay, give the phone back to, Ma, girls."

Without question, Liliana handed the phone back.

"Go get your clothes on," Jordyn told her. "I'll be down to get breakfast ready in a minute."

Liliana went, but Cella stayed behind. Jordyn didn't mind. She tucked her littlest toddler under her arm, and headed out of the bedroom as she stuck the phone between her ear and shoulder.

"Okay, that was a little sad," Jordyn muttered into the phone.

"A little, yeah. Sorry, *bella*."

"Not your fault."

"Kind of."

"Let's not do that, Lucian."

"Hey, that's Dad?"

Jordyn spun on her heels to see her son had finally come out of his room.

Thank God.

John, in all his hazel-eyed, messy-haired glory, stood in the hallway looking like getting out of bed was the last thing he wanted to do. God, he looked like his father. All over. From head to toe. He was already too tall, and getting taller. Already handsome, and puberty hadn't even stepped in to fill him out and roughen him up.

"It is. Do you want to talk to him?" Jordyn asked.

"I only have five more minutes, Jordyn."

That was fine.

More than fine.

A chat with Lucian would do John wonders.

"It's all right," she told her husband. "We have tomorrow."

"All right. Give me to my boy."

She handed the phone over to John, and then he darted back into the safe darkness of his bedroom. Over her shoulder, she called, "Make sure you're dressed before you hang up that phone, John."

"Got it, Ma."

Yep.

Already better.

Chapter 5

December 6ᵗʰ

Jail was a cold slice of hell, Lucian thought. He was a man who cherished his freedom, and jail took it away without a care. A man did not realize how good he had things on the outside, where he could choose his own bedtime, decide what he wanted for meals, and eat when he wanted to. No one understood what it was like to be refused the outdoors and fresh air except for one shitty hour a day.

Never mind the fact he hadn't had a good fuck with his wife for … Jesus, *months*.

Yeah, jail was a special kind of hell.

The only thing that made it even remotely bearable were the visits he got from his family throughout the week. Lucian was grateful for those as they kept him looking forward to the next damn day instead of simply staring at a wall.

It was a good thing he hadn't been put in a prison to serve out his sentence because he wouldn't get as many visits as he did. Honestly, he wasn't sure that he would want his two youngest children—Liliana and Cella—visiting a prison to see him, either. At least with a jail, it was slightly less intimidating.

Prisons, not so much.

"Quiet day," Dante noted.

Lucian rested back in the hard metal chair with a nod. "Seems like it."

"Kind of strange for it being this close to Christmas."

"If I was some of these guys' families, I can't say that I would want to come and visit them, either."

Dante smirked. "I see."

"Is what it is, brother."

"Jordyn been down this week?"

"She's supposed to come on Friday," Lucian said with a shrug, "and bring the girls."

"Not John?"

"Last week, it seemed like he didn't want to come.

Maybe by Friday his mind will have changed. It's hard to say with that kid. He's up and he's down."

"All over the place, really," Dante said.

Lucian nodded. "I did talk to him yesterday. He actually said he missed me. I think this is a big part of his problem."

With those words, Lucian lifted his cuffed hands to the metal table. Dante's gaze dropped to the shiny metal tight to his brother's wrists, and frowned. Getting your ass locked up as a Cosa Nostra man, was always a possibility. A shitty byproduct of their life. That didn't mean they actually wanted to get locked up.

Staying out of jail was always the end-goal.

Still, Lucian saw a flash of something he didn't like to see in his younger brother's eyes. Between the visits with Dante, and the once a week trip Giovanni made to the jail to say hello, it could be taxing.

Dio.

He loved his brothers.

Always would.

Family first.

God second.

But their constant guilt over his current predicament was … tiring. Nobody but Lucian had the illegal gun the day he was pulled over. Given his previous charges and arrests, not to mention his last name and affiliations, the sentence he got was a good sentence.

A light sentence, even.

"You know, I got myself here, right?"

Dante shot his brother a smile. "Sure."

"You also know that you and Giovanni worked some real magic to get my sentence reduced by over seventy-five percent, right?"

A sigh echoed.

"Yeah," Dante said gruffly.

"Then let's just leave it be."

"I can try, but given certain things that are happening, I can't entirely be happy that we didn't get you on a suspended sentence, or some kind of shitty probation. Anything, you know?"

Lucian glanced at his brother. "What the hell do you mean?"

"Pardon?"

"What's happening that I don't know about?"

Dante straightened a bit in his seat, and glanced away. Lucian knew that look on his brother—he knew it damn well. That posture, that hard stare at nothing at all, meant Dante had absolutely zero plans of answering Lucian's questions.

His brother wasn't required to.

Dante was the boss.

Not Lucian.

Their life was all about the respect, after all.

Beyond that, it also might not be very safe for Lucian and Dante to be having too personal, or business-related conversations while in the jail visitation area. There were cameras all over the place, for one damn thing. Guards at the three entrances and exits. Probably a wire somewhere. Hell, maybe the other visitors waiting on detainees weren't even really visitors, but someone planted to listen in on the Marcello brothers.

Dante, the Don. Lucian, his underboss.

Paranoid?

Maybe.

Lucian didn't give a shit. Being paranoid saved his ass more times than he cared to admit. This was just another one of those things. He didn't trust fucking anybody— neither did Dante. It was part of their business, and how they were raised. It wasn't about to change.

It also made this difficult because he really wanted to know what his brother was talking about …

"Are you going to tell me, or tell me to fuck off?" Lucian asked.

Dante chuckled dryly. "The latter, but you know, without the actual words. No need to be rude to you and all, given your … situation."

"Fuck you."

A grin curved his brother's lips.

"Can you tell me?" Lucian pressed after a second.

Dante cleared his throat. "Not really."

"Who knows?"

"Just us brothers, and Papa."

Ah.

"Not even Cat?" Lucian asked, referring to Dante's hellish wife.

Sure, he loved his sister-in-law, but she was still … well, hellish.

"Not even her, but that's only because she hasn't stumbled on something and asked."

"Huh. So, not bad then?"

Dante looked back to Lucian with a wide smile. "Definitely not bad, big brother. Hey, what do you want for Christmas by the way?"

Lucian laughed. "Christmas is going to be long over by the time I get out of here, so don't even worry about it. You don't need to save presents for me, man. I'm good."

"Still. What would you want?"

"Honestly?"

"Yeah."

"To be home with my wife and kids, Dante. What

else?"

Dante nodded. "Thought so. Well, I bought you a new Rolex with black diamonds covering the face of it, so like it and deal with that instead, all right?"

"Are the hands on the watch white?"

"With silver tips," his brother confirmed.

Lucian whistled low. "Damn, I bet that looks good."

"It does."

"Merry Christmas to me."

Dante cocked a brow, but said nothing.

"So hey, if I gave you a note, would you give it to Papa for me?"

"What's the note?" Dante asked.

"A list."

His brother just stared at him.

Lucian rolled his eyes. "Just some things I wanted him to pick up for me—to do."

"Don't make Papa your messenger, Lucian. He's too old for that shit."

What bee crawled up his brother's ass?

"Not a messenger, Dante. He's my *Santa*."

December 9th

Jordyn shot Catrina a look, and then Kim. Neither of her two sisters-in-law said a word as Cecelia continued talking. This was far out of the norm for their mother-in-law. What she was proposing didn't even sound real.

A party.

Them.

Planning it.

Only them planning it.

"So, are you girls up to it?" Cecelia finally asked.

Cella was trying to climb up Jordyn's leg, so she opted to use her daughter as a halfway decent distraction while she answered her mother-in-law. "Of course we can, Cecelia."

"Sure," Cat said right after.

"Uh," Kim deadpanned.

Cecelia's gaze darted to what she probably took as the weakest of the three. The rusty chain. The weak link. The one out of the three girls who was most likely to drop out of the whole shebang. Even if Kim was none of those things.

Her mother-in-law was like a damn shark in the water. She could smell blood from miles away.

Right now, by the look on Cecelia's face, Kim was bleeding out like a gutted pig.

"*Uh*, Kim?" Cecelia asked.

Oh, they loved their mother-in-law. Cecelia Marcello had given them all the most wonderful gifts in the world. Husbands she had raised to be good, decent men. Unconditional love because she treated them like they were her daughters from her body. A mother.

More than anything else, she gave them a mother.

That didn't mean they pretended like their mother-in-law wasn't just a tad bit too anal. That she sometimes got picky on the details. Or that she liked to do all the things only her way.

"Uh," Kim repeated, her gaze darting to her sisters-in-law, and then back to Cecelia just as fast. "You're actually going to let us plan it?"

"Yep," Cecelia said with a nod.

"All of it?"

"That's what I said, Kim."

"Because you're too busy."

"Okay, now you're just parroting stuff back to me, sweetheart. We already went over all of this."

"Because you're going to keep being busy," Kim added, not missing a beat.

"Kim!"

Kim busted out laughing, and in seconds, had everyone else in the room laughing, too. "Hey, it's fine. I was only joking with you, Cecelia. We can have this all planned and ready to go, no worries. Do you have a theme or anything you want to go over with us?"

"I'm letting you three take the reins on everything."

Jordyn gave a little cough. "*Everything?*"

"Every detail. I would prefer that you make homemade food for the guests, but I know we're running short on time. Usually I start prepping for these things a couple of months ahead of time. So this year, cater in."

"Red and white would be a nice theme," Cat joined in with a smile.

"You just have a thing for red," Jordyn told her.

Her oldest sister-in-law didn't even deny it. In fact, Catrina waved her painted red stiletto nails, and her ruby lips curved in a knowing grin. "Well, *sì*, Jordyn."

"A little gold, too, maybe?" Kim asked.

"That would be nice," Cecelia said.

Catrina shrugged. "They did decorate Tuxedo Park in the red and white theme this year, so it would match. We all know Cecelia has a whole attic full of fifty years' worth of Christmas decorations, so we won't be without things to decorate the main rooms for the party."

"*With* new items, please," Cecelia said. "Always with some new items."

Jordyn dictated a few things into her phone, and then looked up at the rest of the women in their family. "So, that's it?"

"Yep." Cecelia didn't look like she entirely believed herself when she said it, but she nodded anyway. Like maybe she was trying to make herself believe what she was saying. "That's it."

"Cecelia, we can handle this," Cat assured.

"No problem," Kim echoed.

"When is the party date?" Jordyn asked. "The one you wanted to have?"

"I was thinking the twentieth."

Jordyn didn't even have to do the math. Her whole

45

life was becoming a ticking clock, counting down minutes, hours, and days until her husband was back home. He wasn't going to be home for the party, or even for Christmas, but she still knew what was coming without having to think on it too hard. She knew because he wasn't going to be there.

Brushing off the sadness that had now taken up residence in her mind and heart, Jordyn said, "Eleven days."

Cecelia frowned. "Not enough time, I think."

Cat shot Jordyn a look that was matched by Kim's.

Shut up, they screamed silently.

Do not get her worked up about this.

"Cecelia, we have got this handled," Jordyn assured.

Somehow.

It was only after the girls were sure that Cecelia was too far from the kitchen to overhear them did they finally get to *really* talking.

"Eleven days," Catrina said to both Jordyn and Kim. "Christmas is five days *after* that. Eleven days."

"It's a little last minute," Jordyn agreed.

Kim waved it all off. "Whatever. We'll delegate some tasks. Each one of us can take a few things to do, and we'll go from there."

"I like that idea."

Cat sighed. "Jordyn, take invitations because you're good with design and colors and all that. Cecelia has a whole list of people with addresses. If you go to that shop in Manhattan, they'll print them and customize envelopes with addresses the same damn day. You'll have to personally mail them, though."

"What's the name of the place?"

Catrina rattled off the store name. Jordyn typed it into her phone.

"Catering will be easier," Kim pointed out.

"I will deal with the caterer," Cat said, "and I will handle some sweets. The least we can do is give Cecelia something homemade, from us, to have at the party. As much as she says she doesn't mind—"

"She does," Jordyn and Kim said in unison.

"Yep."

A few more minutes passed with the girls discussing which tasks were going to who. Once they were done, and satisfied they had this last-minute party handled, Jordyn stood from her chair, ready to get a start on everything.

"By the way," Kim said, looking at Jordyn over her shoulder, "how is Lucian doing?"

"Okay."

Cat made a face as she shrugged on her jacket. "Missing his family, Dante said."

Jordyn swallowed hard. "Yeah, that too."

"When are you going to see him?"

"Antony is supposed to take me and the girls up tomorrow. John hasn't decided if he wants to go or not."

Kim frowned. "Every time he comes over to hang out with Giovanni and Andino, he looks so sad."

"He misses his dad," Jordyn said. "A lot."

"Let us know if you need anything," Catrina told her, "anything at all, Jordyn."

"I'm doing okay."

"Still. Let us know."

"Absolutely," Kim echoed. "I can even take one of the girls, or both of them on a weekend, if you need a break or something."

"And you know Dante will be happy to take John," Cat added.

This was why Jordyn loved her family. Her world had stopped for a short time. Theirs kept moving. They still slowed down to remember her, her struggle, and her kids. It's what family did.

Or, it's what their family did.

Chapter 7

December 10ᵗʰ

"Daddy!"

Lucian looked over his shoulder to see familiar, sweet faces coming his way. Liliana and Cella darted in his direction with matching red chiffon dresses, and shiny black shoes. Jordyn had the girls' hair pulled into high ponytails with matching red bows.

He barely turned in the bench before his girls were on him. Cella, his youngest, climbed into his lap. Liliana jumped onto the bench, then the metal table, and wrapped her little arms around his neck. She hugged for dear life, taking away his ability to breathe.

Jesus.

He didn't even care.

His kids were *everything*.

"Daddy, I missed you!"

Liliana's arms tightened around his neck with her words.

Cella was right up in his face. Her hazel eyes—eyes that matched his—were wide, clear, and happy. "Hi, Dad-day!"

Somehow, he managed to deal with both his girls at the same time. A hand patting Liliana's head, and a kiss to Cella's cheek.

"My girls," Lucian said. "*Ti amo, mia bella caras.* Daddy loves you, my beautiful girls."

Jordyn had finally made her way across the visiting area as well. A soft smile played at the edges of her lips. Lucian looked up at her with a smile and a chuckle. Neither one of the girls had let him go yet, after all, so he couldn't offer her much more.

Unfortunately, the girls didn't get to come to visit as much as he would like for them to. That was a decision made by both him and his wife. Jail was not a place for children. He was lucky enough that when his children did come to visit, the guards agreed to remove his cuffs for the duration.

It saved them explanations to the girls, anyway.

"Hey, *bella*."

Jordyn leaned down enough to give him a quick kiss. "Hey."

"No John?"

Lucian really wanted to see his son. Despite what Jordyn told him on the phone to keep him from worrying about Johnathan, he knew his boy was having trouble. His behavior was already reckless enough for a kid his age, but conversations with his father and brothers let him know John was giving his mother hell.

"No John," Jordyn said with a shrug. "Backed out this morning. Giovanni came to pick him up before we left, said something about gelato and Christmas shopping."

Lucian scoffed. "Giovanni doesn't Christmas shop. He hires someone to do that for him."

"Well, that's what he said."

"John's sad, Daddy," Liliana told him.

Lucian frowned, and patted his daughter's head once more. "Yeah, I know, Lily."

"Santa will make him happy, right?"

Jordyn's gaze found Lucian's, and he really wished they had the right answer for their girl. Neither of them said anything.

What could they say, really?

Cella saved the day by distracting them all. "I pees by myself now!"

Lucian's eyes stretched wide at her exclamation, and a laugh burst from his lips. Kids had no concept of privacy, or filters. Little milestones that their parents made big deals out of often became sentiments they repeated to others in public, so they too could share in the wonder.

Being embarrassed was a part of being a parent.

"Do you?" he asked her.

"Only took three months," Jordyn told him with a roll of her pretty eyes.

"Only, huh?"

"That, and a package of princess underwear she found at the store one day. She was determined not to mess in them. I wish I had known that trick years ago for the other two."

Lucian chuckled. "Maybe you'll be able to use it once more for another at some point, *dolcezza*."

Jordyn gave him a look. "Ah, no. You've knocked me up enough times, thanks."

"Jord."

"Nope."

They had decided they were done having kids. Jordyn even had some weird looking birth control put in that was basically ninety-nine-point-nine percent effective. It could last up to eight years without anyone doing anything. Or it was supposed to, anyway.

Lucian called that shit a lifesaver.

He still might like one more.

Another boy, maybe.

But his *principessas* were perfect, too.

Another girl would be fine.

He just had to work on Jordyn …

"Do you misses me, Daddy?" Liliana asked.

Lucian's attention went back to his oldest girl in an instant. "Of course, I miss you."

"Will you come home soon?"

Jordyn plucked her daughter off the table, and sat down on the metal bench beside her husband. Liliana sat in her mother's lap, and Cella rested happily in his. "Soon, Lily. Daddy will be home soon."

They were so young.

They couldn't possibly understand.

Lucian supposed he knew why it was more difficult for John to come see his father. The boy was several years older than his sisters, and understood a great deal more about their current situation. He probably blamed his father for being where he was, and frankly, had every damn right to. A conversation with his boy over the phone was easy—they could both pretend Lucian was not where he actually was. A face to face visit was not quite the same.

At least, John had his uncles and grandfather for the moment.

More lifesavers.

"Daddy," Cella said, turning in his lap to peer up at him again, "guess what?"

"What, *bambina*?"

"We has big Crit-mah tree."

"Really?"

"*Eva*," she said with a dramatic nod and big eyes.

"Wow."

"Mmhmm."

Lucian looked to his wife with a grin. "And I bet Ma had so much fun putting that up, too."

Jordyn made a sound under her breath, and glanced upward. "Fun, right."

"The girls love it, though."

"That's the only reason it didn't go straight out the back door."

Lucian laughed.

This was what he needed.

A visit from his girls, and his wife. His mood was instantly better. His outlook finally improved. He probably wouldn't see the girls again for a visit until after the holiday season, so he really just wanted to soak this one up for all it was worth.

"Love you, Jordyn," he told his wife.

She smiled at him, reached out, and stroked his cheek with her palm. "Love you, Lucian."

December 12th

Jordyn balanced the phone between her shoulder and ear as she dug the party invitations from her purse. They had all of eight days to get these invitations to the people who needed them. Of course, she didn't think for a second that any person who got an invitation to the Marcello Christmas party would refuse, but they were kind of running short on time.

With a stack of envelops in hand, she moved to the back of the line inside the large post office. Her sister-in-law chatted away in her ear.

"He's just …"

"What?" Jordyn asked.

"In such a *mood*," Catrina muttered.

"Really?"

"I know, it's not like Dante at all."

Not really, no. To outsiders, sure. Dante Marcello could come off as cold, aloof, and distant. It was his own way of protecting his family. To his wife, kids, and anyone inside their family? Dante was far warmer.

"He's snapping at every little thing," Catrina admitted.

Jordyn frowned. "Maybe he needs a break, Cat."

"Life is a bit too busy for breaks, isn't it?"

"We all need them occasionally."

"Sure, but how do I explain that to my very difficult, stubborn husband who wakes up at five every morning, runs for an hour on the treadmill, drinks his coffee by seven sharp, and has the rest of his day planned out by the *hour*?"

Jordyn let out a little laugh.

Catrina had a point.

"Well, I don't know. I suppose that's something you'll have to figure out."

"You're no help, Jordyn."

"Hey, I am just trying to get these damn invitations out for the party on time. Don't ask for too much from me right now. I'll probably end up missing Lucian's call today, actually. This line is *so* long."

"Sorry." Catrina made a noise under her breath. "Bad time of year, I suppose. Everyone is busy, and rushing."

"Cecelia does this every year, though."

"She does, but she's also done it for three decades, Jordyn."

"Truth."

"I'll let you go. I need to get on the phone with the caterer, anyway. Finish up those details. At least it's a caterer Cecelia likes."

Jordyn snorted. "Yes, when it's *other* people's parties."

"I think she'll just be happy to have a party at all this year."

Well, that's what they were all hoping, really.

"All right. Call me later if you need to rant about Dante again," Jordyn said.

Catrina laughed lowly. "Will do."

"*MA!*"

The girlish screech on the other end of the phone made Jordyn wince. Good God, Catherine had a set of lungs on her. Everybody in their family thought the girl was a lot like her mother, but louder and with a touch of her father to color her up.

No one dared to tell Catrina that her daughter was

just like her, though.

"Okay, the *principessa* calls," Catrina said with a sigh.

"Give her kisses for me."

"Will do."

Jordyn hung up with her sister-in-law, and then checked the line. She had barely moved at all. In fact, there were four lines altogether, and every single one of them went all the way back to the front of the building. Four more people had come in to stand behind Jordyn. Almost everyone in front of her had a box filled with stuff to mail.

Presents, likely.

Catrina was right.

This *was* a busy time of year.

Oh, well.

Jordyn didn't have much of a choice but to wait. She would definitely be missing Lucian's call, though. That made her a little sad.

She was still counting down her days.

Waiting on him ...

• • •

Jordyn groaned in relief as she kicked off the heeled boots in the entryway of her home. She nudged the toe-killers into the corner, and vowed never to wear the damn

59

things again if she knew standing for long periods of time was a good possibility. Her feet ached, and her toes felt like they were broken.

She swore the bigger the price tag on a pair of shoes, the more uncomfortable they could be. Yet, she loved the stupid things enough to keep buying them.

Plus, they made her legs look great.

After she put her bag and coat away, Jordyn headed for the kitchen. She found the phone blinking with a missed call. The familiar number made her frown.

The jail.

Still, it seemed Lucian had left a message. She opted to listen to it now and if everything was okay, she could play it for the kids later once they got back from Giovanni and Kim's place. Hitting the play button, Lucian's voice filtered through the speaker.

"Missed you again, Jordyn. Let the kids know I love them. I'll call tomorrow. I hope they like the early surprise Santa left for them and you. Ciao, amore."

Jordyn's brow furrowed.

What surprise?

Nothing had looked out of place in the entryway, and not in the kitchen. Her front door had still been locked when she finally got back home from the post office. She had no idea what Lucian was talking about, but she supposed that was probably his point.

She would figure it out later.

While she had the house to herself for a little bit, she had other things to do. Pick up toys, vacuum floors, and strip some beds. The chores never ended, really. They had a twice a week maid, but that was only because Lucian got irritated when Jordyn tried to do everything herself. She got irritated when the maid tried to do more than Jordyn wanted her to.

It was a delicate line.

She headed for the living room to pick up the mess of toys Cella had left earlier in the day. She only took one step inside the space, and froze right where she stood.

When she left that morning, their Christmas tree had been empty underneath it. All of the kids' presents were safely locked away in her walk-in closet, needing to be wrapped and labeled. Some from her and Lucian, and some from *Santa*.

Now, however, what had been bare space under the Christmas tree was full of gifts. Small, and big. Gold, red, silver, and blue wrapping papers. Long boxes, a couple of bags with tissue paper sticking out of the top, and ribbons tied to each gift. A bow accompanied each gift, too.

Jordyn stepped forward, and reached for a folded up card that rested on one of the bigger gifts. Opening it, she found a sweet note staring back at her.

Merry Christmas, Marcellos.

Santa had to help Daddy this year.

We hope you don't mind!

XOXO

Jordyn smiled, and held the card a little tighter between the tips of her fingers. She recognized the handwriting on the card as her father-in-law's. Antony was one of the few people who did have access to their home with a spare key.

Wow, Jordyn thought as she looked over the gifts.

Lucian figured out a way to help and kind of be present, after all.

December 19th

The clang of metal on metal had Lucian's eyes popping open. For the most part, the jail was quiet. He was in a single cell with no bunkmate, and he liked that just fine. Sometimes, the occasional drunk was brought in during the late evening or early morning hours. The sounds of their grumblings or whatever else could be annoying, but nothing too bad.

Certainly not like prison.

That place was a special kind of hell. Lucian would deal with the slight annoyances of jail.

"You up in there, Marcello, or what?"

Lucian blinked at the stucco ceiling. "I am now."

He didn't even bother to look at the guard who had woken him up. He knew them all by name, now. Usually, the guards treated him with a healthy respect.

And for good reason, he supposed. His last name afforded him that kind of peace.

There were, however, a couple of special guards that took great pleasure in smirking at him from behind the bars. As though they were taunting him in their minds.

He ignored that shit, too.

Mostly because the bastards never had the balls to open their mouths and actually *say* something.

"Get up, we gotta transfer ya, man."

The guard's heavy Brooklyn accent reminded Lucian of his younger years. It brought back memories of his father—his biological father, not his adoptive one. Time and life and privilege had all but drained his family's old inflections.

His bio-father … in his memories … always sounded like a Brooklyn native, though.

"Are you getting up, or what?" the guard asked.

Lucian sighed, and rolled over on the metal bed. His back protested every single fucking movement. He felt twice his age because of this place. That was another shitty thing about being in lockup. Another thing to add to his pile that he missed about being back home.

The bed was a piece of garbage. The mattress—if you could even call it that—was nothing more than a one-inch piece of foam covered by a scratchy sheet. It did nothing to soften the hard surface beneath it. The pillow was some plastic covered nonsense, and equally as thin as the mattress. The blanket it came with?

Also garbage.

It *was* jail, though.

Lucian stopped complaining because what was the point? He had gotten himself here, after all. It was what it was.

Standing up, Lucian eyed the guard outside the cell as he stretched his limbs. The small cell did little to satisfy his need to move, be active, and shake off the general restlessness inside his mind and body.

The guard rolled his eyes as Lucian turned on the faucet to the sink, and grabbed a handful of water to cup to his mouth for a drink.

"You're sure draggin' your ass today, huh?"

Lucian shrugged. "Nowhere to be but here at the moment, man."

"Sure, sure."

"Transfer, you said?"

The guard nodded. "Yep. Or something like that. I

don't know, I'm not given a lot of details on what's working, Lucian. I just take you to where I am told to."

"All right."

Lucian stepped up to the cell, and put his hands through the slot. Quickly, the guard slapped on a pair of cuffs, and waved for him to step back again. Once he had, the bars were unlocked and opened, allowing Lucian the illusion of freedom.

Next to his hour a day outside to blow off some steam—not that it was worth anything being as cold as it was—he didn't leave his cell.

"You gotta see the judge, I guess," the guard told him.

Lucian cocked a brow. "The judge?"

The guard shrugged. "I just deliver you where you gotta go, Marcello. I told you that."

Right, right.

• • •

Lucian allowed the officer to help him from the back of the cruiser. High above his head, plastered to the white brick of a building, he read the name of the courthouse. He still didn't have the first damn clue about what was going on.

He requested to call his lawyer. The cop told him that he wouldn't need to. He asked for details on what was happening. Nothing was explained.

Lucian was starting to dislike this more and more. He couldn't help it. His very nature was to be suspicious and paranoid.

That shit saved his life.

"One step ahead of me, Marcello," the cop demanded, "and no funny business, either."

Lucian gave the guy a look.

Who the fuck did he think he was dealing with?

Lucian knew how this shit went.

"Let's go," the cop said. "I'll tell you where to go once we're inside."

Lucian did as he was told. Once inside the building, they went through security and the metal detectors. He glowered at a female security guard as she patted him down, and came a little too close for comfort to his junk.

"Been a while?" the woman asked him with a smile.

"Keep touching me," Lucian told her, "and I'll let my wife know the name and number on your badge."

The woman stepped back.

Lucian only smiled at her.

"Be nice, Marcello," the cop said as he was taken down another set of hallways. "This is supposed to be a good day for you, or something like that."

What?

Lucian didn't even bother to ask.

A few minutes, and an elevator ride later, Lucian stared at the name of a judge printed on a cherry-stained door.

Chambers of the Honorable Judge Theodore Nolaw.

"I seriously fucking hope I wasn't dragged out of my cell today for some set up with Feds, or nonsense like that," Lucian grumbled. "Waste of your damn time, as you all have already been told."

The cop chuckled.

He was kind of serious.

It wouldn't be the first time they had pulled that shit on him. Like they thought getting a few months in lock up was somehow going to shake the fear into his bones, and put him on the path of right in his life.

Bullshit.

God hadn't done that.

Jail time hadn't done that.

Nothing was going to do that.

He liked being who he was, even if that person lived in the gray of life, never entirely good, but never entirely bad, either.

"I will be waiting out here to unlock your cuffs once

you're finished with your meeting," the cop said.

Lucian should have taken that as his first clue today was going to be a good day for him. Instead, he got distracted by the man waiting inside the judge's chambers as the door was opened for him.

Giovanni.

His brother.

His lawyer.

"Care for a get out of jail free card?" Gio asked.

Lucian smirked. "Pulled that out of your ass, did you?"

"Gotta save my tricks for the bad ones, man."

Damn.

He loved his brother.

"Antony is going to owe me *big time* for this one," the judge muttered behind his desk.

Lucian cocked an eyebrow as the door was closed behind him. Apparently, he should also be thanking his father.

He wasn't surprised.

Chapter 10

December 20th

"Oh, you girls did *wonderful*."

Jordyn smiled at her mother-in-law's praise. "We really did try, Cecelia."

"I know. And I did shove it on you all last minute, didn't I?"

"A little," Jordyn said with a laugh.

Cecelia shrugged, and spun a small circle in the great hall of the Marcello mansion. It made the skirt of her deep green dress spin wide around her legs, and showed off the kitten heels she wore. Even at her age, Cecelia still liked to wear heels. It always made Jordyn smile.

"Yes, well, no matter. You all did amazing. Look at this place."

Jordyn had.

A lot.

Several times over the past few days.

The final details of the Christmas party had come together fantastically. It helped that each of the girls—her, Kim, and Catrina—each fulfilled their duties, and without issue or complaint. Nothing was left hanging. Everything fell into place just so.

The decorations were up.

A live tree was in every room.

Lights twinkled.

Hot food was waiting.

Jordyn and Cecelia stepped to the side as servers carrying trays moved from the kitchen through the great hall. The hired staff moved quietly between spaces as they readied for guests. They didn't seem to need much help with their jobs.

For that, Jordyn was grateful.

As it was, the girls still had enough to handle on their own. Greeting guests. Making sure every single little thing planned for the night went off without a hitch. Keeping Cecelia placated and happy so that she would trust them more often with parties and the like.

71

Cecelia eyed one of the trays with sweets as the last of the servers passed them by. "I tried one of those earlier."

Jordyn gave her mother-in-law a look. "Cecelia."

"I had to try the food, now."

"Seriously."

Cecelia waved a hand. "I *had* to. It's very good, by the way."

Jordyn hid her smile by taking a sip of water she had been nursing for a half hour. It was supposed to be her time for a break, after all.

"Is that so?" she asked.

"Quite good."

"Even for *catering*?"

Cecelia rolled her eyes upward. "Well, I do know you girls cooked a bit."

"We did."

"But the catering is also good, Jordyn."

She let her smile bloom in full force at that, not bothering to hide it a bit. Despite all of the reservations Cecelia had seemed to have for this party, Jordyn was pleased to see the woman was impressed, and enjoying herself.

So far.

The guests had yet to arrive.

Speaking of which …

Jordyn checked her watch.

"Just about time, isn't it?" Cecelia asked.

Jordyn nodded. "Just about. Cars will be coming up the drive soon enough."

Cecelia turned to look over the only tree in the great hall. It stood tall at over twenty feet. The top damn near grazed the crystal chandelier hanging from the ceiling. The girls had opted for a different color scheme in each space where the guests would be using for the party. The main room was blue and silver. The kitchen, gold. The entertainment room, green and red.

The main hall?

White and red.

The large tree was all decked out in the Christmas colors. White twinkle lights flashed along with the music that pumped out from the sound system at a low level. Instead of traditional Christmas carols, they had opted for a more choir feel in their choices.

From the living room, Jordyn could hear the kids laughing and playing with toys. Gifts that their grandparents had allowed them to open early.

"Everything is perfect," Cecelia said, smiling to herself.

Even as she said that, Jordyn thought she heard an echo of sadness in her mother-in-law's tone. She wasn't entirely sure, but she didn't want Cecelia upset in any way. This was intended to be a good, happy, and relaxing day for her.

"Something is wrong," Jordyn said. "So what is it, Cecelia?"

"Oh, nothing."

"Just tell me. I'm sure I could fix it. We've got …" Jordyn checked her watch again. "Well, like three minutes. But hey, have faith. What is it?"

Cecelia laughed quietly, and turned to pat her daughter-in-law on the cheek with a soft, gentle palm. "Nothing, dear. I was just thinking it would have been nice to have Lucian here, that's all. He likes Christmas—it's the only holiday he does care for. But … what can you do?"

Jordyn's own happiness deflated a bit.

She couldn't help it.

"Apparently, we can't always get what we want for Christmas," Jordyn murmured.

Cecelia sighed. "No, we cannot."

"Cecelia, I am not wearing this damn Santa hat!"

Antony's shout echoed from somewhere upstairs on the second level. Cecelia gave Jordyn a little wink before heading in the direction of her husband's voice.

Jordyn already knew …

Cecelia would win that battle.

Antony should have known better.

• • •

At the front doors of the mansion, Jordyn stood with her sisters-in-law to greet the guests as they came into the mansion, and hand over a gift. Each gift bag held a gold-flaked Christmas ornament with Swarovski crystals inside, specialty chocolates imported from France, and a few other favorite things Cecelia had picked out.

"Ma, is it okay if we play in the second wing?"

Jordyn turned away from a guest she had been greeting to reply to her oldest daughter. Liliana looked sweet as could be in her gold and white dress. Somehow—for unknown reasons that Jordyn was grateful—her daughter had managed to stay clean. She could not say the same for Cella, but one thing at a damn time.

Plus, John had also been in a good mood all day.

Another check in Jordyn's favor.

It was the small things, after all.

"Can we?" Liliana asked.

Jordyn's distraction was handled by Kim stepping in to greet the next guest, so Liliana could be taken care of. Bending down to talk to her daughter, Jordyn had her back to the door. Cold air blew over her body as the door was opened again.

"Well, do you think you should play in the other wing?" Jordyn asked. "We're supposed to be saying hello to everyone, and having a party, Liliana."

"I know, Ma."

"So … maybe later?"

Liliana didn't answer. Her gaze darted over her mother's shoulder, and then upward at someone behind Jordyn.

Jordyn didn't know *why*, but she just knew who was standing there.

Maybe it was her daughter's growing smile.

Maybe it was his shadow overtaking them.

Maybe it was her suddenly racing heart, and thrumming soul.

Lucian.

"Merry Christmas, Jordyn," he said.

December 20th

"Daddy!"

Liliana's squeal could have broken glass from the high pitch. Lucian didn't even mind. His wife stood and spun on her heel with wide, sea-blue eyes finding his hazel gaze. All he needed was a single look from Jordyn—her love always stared back at him—and everything was right and good in his world once more.

"Lucian," Jordyn said.

Whispered was more like it.

She stared at him, unmoving.

She didn't even blink.

"You *are* seeing what you think you're seeing," he told her.

Her smile bloomed wide.

Honest, pure, and good.

So beautiful.

Instantly, his wife lurched forward. Lucian already had his arms wide open to catch her in his embrace. He was vaguely aware of the onlookers surrounding them. Guests for a party that, according to his brother, their wives had been working on nonstop for the whole month.

Lucian didn't care at all.

Not when Jordyn kissed him.

Her hands fisted into his suit jacket to drag him impossibly closer. His lips melded against hers in a familiar dance that always left him hot as hell and happy in his heart.

This woman was his soul.

Every good part of it.

"Daddy, you're here!"

Liliana hugged Lucian's legs. His oldest daughter's excitement was the only reason he pulled away from his wife. Jordyn didn't seem to mind, but he promised himself they would get back to what they were doing soon enough.

Later was waiting, after all.

Bending down, Lucian let his fingers drift through the

free, dark waves of Liliana's hair. "Hey, *principessa*. Love you."

Liliana's cheeks pinked in her joy. "Did Santa bring you home?"

Lucian passed Jordyn a look. She only shrugged.

"Kind of," Lucian said.

"And you'll be home all of Christmas, too?"

Lucian nodded. "Yes, I will."

"Yay!"

"Dad!"

"*Dad-day!*"

Apparently, word had already traveled about his arrival. Lucian barely got the chance to blink before he was tackled from the side by his two other kids.

Cella practically hung around his middle. John grabbed his father from behind around the neck. They took him to the floor, and like a fucking football team, piled on top of him until he was smothered by his kids. He couldn't even breathe.

Lucian didn't mind.

Not at all.

• • •

"Oh, my boy," Cecelia said, kissing Lucian on both

cheeks. "I am so very happy you're here."

Usually, he didn't let people fawn over him like this. Certainly not to the extent Cecelia was doing. Still, she was his mother, and he loved her.

Entirely.

Plus, his father was standing just a couple of feet behind Cecelia with a stare that told Lucian he was *not* to move an inch until his mother was done. Antony had always been like that where his wife was concerned; he made sure she was happy, no matter what. Lucian supposed that was why he and his brothers were the same way with their wives at the end of the day.

"Let me get a good look at you," his mother demanded.

Cecelia looked him all over, checking for any sign of injury or distress.

"Ma," Lucian said.

Cecelia hushed him.

Again, she continued her search.

"Ma, I am *fine*."

"I know, but still, Lucian."

Out of the corner of his eye, Lucian kept watch on his wife. His son and daughters had darted off somewhere to play with their cousins again. Once they had been convinced that their father actually wasn't going anywhere.

Lucian hadn't been able to fully appreciate seeing his wife after months of only getting a half hour visit here and there. Jordyn looked damn good in a gold dress that hugged her curves, and showed off her legs. She had let her hair down in loose curls—a style he loved just because it gave him something to play with.

Motherhood and life had changed his wife, but in the best of ways. A little curvier in her hips. Thicker in her thighs. New lines and curves and *more* for him to love. And he did. God, did he love every inch of her.

The strappy gold heels on her feet definitely added to the appeal her legs already had. The heels made them look longer, and likely better if they were wrapped around his—

"So how did you manage this, huh?" his mother asked.

Lucian was brought out of his less than innocent thoughts to answer his mother's question. He had to clear his throat and remind himself now was not the time. *Soon*, but not now.

Tugging up his pant leg, Lucian showed his mother the blinking black box that was attached to his ankle. Quickly, he dropped his pants to hide the ankle monitor once more.

"House arrest for the next couple of months," he said with a chuckle. "However, *someone* …" Lucian nodded to his father, adding, "And someone else—not saying who, but it was Gio—pulled some strings and got permission for me to attend the party tonight, and be here for Christmas morning."

Cecelia put a hand over her heart. "So you just got out today?"

"Early this morning. All last night was paperwork. It took longer than we thought. I spent the night in a waiting room until my monitor was ready and everything was signed off. I went to the house when I knew Jordyn was here to have a shower, and put a decent suit on."

"But you're *here*."

"I am, Ma. Merry Christmas."

Cecelia's soft smile lit up her whole face. "Merry Christmas, my boy. I couldn't have asked for a better gift than you."

• • •

Jordyn's tinkling laughter filled the empty hallway of the Marcello mansion. She tried to tug on his grasp to slow him down, but Lucian just kept pulling her along.

"There is a party downstairs!" she told him.

"About to be one up here, too."

"Lucian, I'm supposed to be *hosting*."

She was going to be hosting something else, too.

Quick, fast, and in a hurry.

"Where are we going?" she asked.

Lucian didn't answer, simply slipped into a familiar room and shut the door behind them. He didn't give Jordyn much of a chance to look around his old bedroom—it was a blast from the past, anyway. His mother never changed things. She never updated the space. She kept the floor clean, and the sheets fresh.

Just in case.

"What—"

Lucian effectively quieted his wife's questions, and her laughter, with a bruising kiss. At the same time, he backed her into the door, using his body to confine her against him. Jordyn laughed into his kiss, and pushed all of her sweet, sinful curves into his hard lines. He kissed her until his lips were numb and his lungs begged for air.

His hands couldn't be controlled. Exploring his wife's body, driving over the shimmering, body-hugging dress she wore, and then edging beneath the skirt to drive the material higher. He heard the lock on the bedroom door click, and realized Jordyn had been the one to do it.

Good.

She knew what he wanted.

She was up for it.

Perfect.

"You've got fifteen minutes," his wife murmured against his throat. "Fifteen, Lucian, and that's all. I have to be back downstairs. I promised."

"Fifteen minutes works for me."

Besides, he'd have all damn night once he got his wife home.

Jordyn squeaked with surprise when Lucian yanked her away from the door. The bed was a few feet away—a large thing that gave him lots of space and comfort to move. He ended up sitting his wife down on the edge of the fucking dresser.

It worked.

Plus, if he got Jordyn in a bed, there was no telling how long they would stay there. She did say fifteen minutes, after all. He was going to try to stick to that.

"God, I missed you," Jordyn hummed as Lucian kissed from his wife's chin down the column of her delicate throat. He could feel her heartbeat thrumming under his lips and tongue. She tasted like she always did— sweet, sexy, and all his. "Would you hurry the hell up and fuck me already?"

"You're impatient."

"You made me this way."

He had.

Lucian regretted nothing.

His hands skimmed under his wife's skirt, found the edges of lace panties, and pulled. She lifted from the dresser just enough to help him get those panties down her legs. He tucked them in his back pocket as she yanked her skirt up around her hips.

"Fuck," Lucian groaned.

Legs spread open.

Pretty pussy.

Grinning, painted red smile.

Sex.

Sin.

Love.

The sight in front of Lucian was the best damn thing he had ever seen, as far as he was concerned.

"Merry Christmas to me," he said.

Jordyn's smile turned even more sinful. "It certainly will be. Get back here, *now*."

Lucian didn't need to be told a second time. His wife helped to undo his pants, and get them shoved down around his hips. Her hands dipped beneath his boxer-briefs, and with a few firm strokes, his already semi-hard cock was ready to be balls-deep in her wet, tight cunt.

Jordyn's cupped his face and brought him in for another searing kiss as he finally slid home inside his wife.

He found heaven there.

He found bliss there.

He found life there.

"Holy fuck, yeah," Lucian breathed against his wife's mouth.

Jordyn kissed him again. "You're down to at least eleven minutes, Lucian."

He wasn't moving.

Her pussy hugged him so tight, it was hard to breathe.

"Don't care," he said.

Her lips grazed his cheek, and jaw. Her fingernails dragged soft lines over his exposed skin. All of it felt too fucking good to be true, but he knew it was.

It all came to a head when she whispered his name— soft and needy—in his ear. He couldn't take it anymore. He couldn't *not* move anymore.

Lucian stroked his thumb over Jordyn's red lips while he pounded into her. Her soft cries filled the quiet space, and urged him on faster. She sucked his digit into her mouth, and *fuck* …

Life was good again. Their life was always good.

Yeah.

Merry Christmas to him.

Dante & Catrina

December 9th

Catrina Marcello had never been much of a holidays or Christmas person until she had a reason to be. Mainly, once she was married, settled, and had kids. Before all of that, the holidays simply came and went.

It was just another day in her already busy year. She didn't make time to do anything special for it because back then, she hadn't needed to.

Now, though?

Catrina loved it.

Her son and daughter helped a lot with that, honestly.

The closer Christmas came, the more excited they became. Michel was at an age where he no longer believed in Santa thanks to a few older kids at school who broke the news.

However, Catherine, their youngest and only biological child still very much believed in the magic of Christmas. Catrina had kept a little bit of the magic alive for Michel by having him *help* set up Catherine's Santa things.

It worked.

It was also the only time of year when Catrina really stopped to slow down and enjoy the things happening around her fully. Throughout the rest of the year, she was so incredibly busy between work, family, and everything else.

It was only Christmas and New Year when she had no guilt about clearing her schedule, turning off the phones, and whatever else she needed to do for her kids and husband to be entirely present.

There with them.

Only them.

This year, on the other hand, was turning out to be less pleasant than years past. Not because of her, but rather, her husband.

Already, she could hear Dante's anger and frustration becoming louder, and leaking down the hall. Catrina stood at the other end, and listening to her husband bark at someone on a phone call—likely one of his men, but she couldn't be sure.

If the past month or so were any indication, Dante would only get progressively louder and louder until he woke everyone up in the goddamn house. Catrina didn't want Michel and Catherine woken up by their father's yelling.

Dante wasn't typically a loud man. He rarely had bad moods. Lately it was an everyday kind of thing. The smallest thing could set him into some kind of a fit. Never to her or their kids, of course, but still.

Catrina didn't know what in the hell was up with her husband. Dante was masterful at balancing his responsibilities between his family life, and business life. After doing it for almost a decade with no issues, these new moods and problems were a bit concerning.

He was her perfect match—a loving yet challenging husband. He was the *best* father, a fantastic boss when it came to his crime organization, and he never missed a click.

Until recently.

He was struggling.

Catrina didn't know how to help.

She figured the best thing to do for the moment

would be to leave Dante alone to his phone call. She headed up to the third floor of their large Amityville home to where Catherine and Michel's bedrooms were situated.

A quick check on Michel told Catrina the boy was sleeping away. An *I Survived* book was still overturned on his extra pillow. It wasn't unusual for Michel to fall asleep reading. He was incredibly book smart—apparently that was a thing. He much preferred reading, learning, and school to friends, playing, and whatever else.

Catherine, on the other hand, was still wide awake in her bed.

Not a surprise.

Catrina leaned in the doorway of her almost five-year-old's room. Catherine pretended to be asleep when she noticed her mother peering in on her.

"I can see you're not sleeping, Catherine."

"I am, Ma."

"Then why are you talking?"

Catherine giggled. "Sorry, Ma."

"Go to sleep."

"I had to pee."

"Okay, but now you have to sleep. Santa is coming, and we have to be a good girl. Right?"

Catherine nodded. "Right, Ma."

"Night, *reginella*."

"Night, Ma."

Since at least one of their kids happened to still be awake, Catrina decided to head back down to Dante. After all, she could still hear him raging away on the phone. Probably to the same guy he had been yelling at when she was down there the first damn time.

Catrina stood in the doorway of her husband's office while he finished his phone call. She didn't say anything, and he didn't notice her there as his back was turned.

"No, you make sure that shit is done the way I told you to have it done …" Dante paused, and his shoulders stiffened as he listened to whatever reply came back to his statement. Catrina swore she could *see* the knot of tension forming between his shoulder blades through his dress shirt. "I don't have time for this fucking nonsense. Get. It. Done."

Dante slammed down the phone on his desk, but just as quickly, he picked it back up again. He dialed another number without ever turning around to see Catrina standing there watching him. A couple of seconds after he put the phone to his ear, he started talking.

"Yeah, Gio? I need an update on the Lucian thing."

Wonderful.

Now her husband was about to go ballistic on his brother because he had taken all the hits he could on the last punching bag of the day. Catrina rubbed at her temples, willing the oncoming headache to back off for a few more minutes.

"Well find out, Gio!"

Dante's shout echoed.

Catrina winced.

Okay, that's quite enough.

She strolled into the room, snatched the phone from her husband's hand, and turned her back to him as he spun to face her. She did catch the sight of his pissed off scowl, but she had other things to handle at the moment.

Catrina put the phone to her ear. "Gio?"

"What crawled up his fucking ass?" her brother-in-law asked.

"If someone figures it out, tell them to let me know," Catrina replied dryly.

"He needs to relax."

"I'm aware, Gio."

"Give me the goddamn phone, Cat."

Catrina held up a hand over her shoulder, but otherwise, said nothing to her husband. She went back to Gio instead. "He will call you back tomorrow. How does that sound?"

"You make it tomorrow night, and I will make sure your Christmas gift is *extra* awesome," Gio replied.

Catrina laughed. "Deal."

The phone call clicked off.

Catrina set the phone to the receiver, and turned to face her glowering husband. Every single inch of him radiated a pissed off atmosphere. It was damn near impossible for her to stand close to him and not also get defensive simply because of his posture.

"Go do something else, *bello*," Catrina told him.

Dante's green gaze narrowed. "I beg your pardon?"

She pointed at the door. "Get out of this office. Go have a coffee. A shower. Run on the treadmill. Beat the shit out of your punching bag. I really don't care, but if you keep yelling my walls down while you're on the phone, we're going to have a problem."

Dante didn't move.

Neither did Catrina.

Finally, her husband said, "I have work to do, Cat."

"Nothing that cannot wait, *bello*."

"Says you."

"So be it."

Dante let out a grunt of frustration.

Catrina still held her ground.

Then, she pointed at the door again. "Go do something else."

Dante went.

Catrina let out a sigh of relief.

One battle down.

A million more to go.

December 10th

The front door slammed under Dante Marcello's heavy hand. Usually, he wouldn't be doing that kind of shit, but damn, lately he needed some kind of an outlet for the irritation that just kept building higher and higher.

As a crime boss, it was no longer acceptable for him to use physical violence when he needed or wanted something done. He was expected to act as an example for his men, and behave accordingly. He was meant to *talk*. Talk like it was his friend, talk like it was fine, and talk until he got what he wanted done.

Just fucking talk.

Dante was so done with talking at this point that it wasn't even funny.

Perhaps if all he had to worry about was talking, it wouldn't be such a goddamn issue. It wasn't *just* his Cosa Nostra, though. It was his legal business, too. Work that just kept piling up. Issues that kept weeding their way through cracks he couldn't fill.

Nonstop nonsense.

Frustrated that yet another work day had left him with more things added onto his to-do list, and nothing actually solved. He should've been happy to be home. Except he wasn't.

Dante was a lot of things—stubborn, difficult, and particular.

He was not, however, an idiot.

His problems with work outside of the house had started to bleed into his home and family life. He saw it every day he came home—like today—and his kids didn't greet him at the door. Never mind his wife, who was probably just about at her wits end where he was concerned, too.

Dante shrugged off his jacket, and eyed the empty hallway. The best part of his days was this moment right here … or, it should be.

His kids didn't come running. His wife wasn't waiting

at the end of the hallway. He barely heard a sound other than the faint hum of the television in another room.

Cinnamon and sugar clung to the air as he put his shoes into the rack. Fresh pine wafted through the living room entryway as he passed it by. Compliments of the tree he had gotten a man to pick up and bring to his home.

All the scents of Christmas.

It should have been the most wonderful time of the year.

Wasn't that what the song said?

Right.

Fucking joke.

Dante hadn't gotten five damn minutes this year to even enjoy the season. He hadn't been able to shop for his wife or kids—never mind his brothers, their wives, or his parents—other than some online browsing. At some point, those online purchases would be delivered to his house, but it was looking like he would have to pay someone else to wrap the damn things for him.

Yeah, it sucked.

Usually, he would help his wife decorate. *He* would be the one to grab their tree while Michel tagged along to demand it be perfect all around. He would hang the high ornaments, and lift Catherine up to put the angel on top.

Not this year.

All of that had been done without him. Not by his choice, of course, but it was still done.

And Cat!

Catrina *cooked*—she cooked the best things around this time of year, and Dante barely got to taste any of it.

He fucking *hated* it.

Dante supposed that wasn't helping with his mood, either. He felt like he was missing out on something that usually made his kids and wife happy. He wasn't there to help them, or watch their excitement grow as Christmas came closer.

Add on his mood to make them wary, and it was just crappy all around.

Dante found his wife in the kitchen. Catrina didn't look up at his entrance, and instead, focused on the book she was reading while she sipped what looked to be hot chocolate from her favorite mug. He could smell hints of peppermint, too, so it was probably one of those specialty ones she liked.

In the kitchen, the scents of cinnamon and sugar were far heavier. It almost made his mouth water, but he had other things on his mind at the moment.

"Where are the kids?"

"Hello to you, too," Catrina murmured, never looking away from her book.

Dante's gaze narrowed. "Evening, Cat. My day was shit. How was yours?"

"Fine."

"Until now, right?"

At his unneeded, rude response, Catrina set her cup down, closed her book, and slowly turned in her seat to face Dante. He didn't need to be told by her to know he had crossed a line with what he said.

Still, it was out there now.

He couldn't take it back.

"Excuse me, *bello*?" Catrina asked calmly.

He always liked how even when she was raging pissed—which she clearly was *now*—how she could both let her tone cut him with its sharpness while also calling him handsome. She did it without batting a lash.

"Your day," Dante said, wondering what in the hell he was doing and where in the fuck he planned to go with this. "I bet it was a lot better before I got home, huh?"

Catrina cocked a brow.

Dante didn't back down. "It's like the kids, too. I come home, and they're anywhere but here lately. Upstairs in their rooms, outside, or wherever else. As long as it's not next to me, then they don't care. Right?"

"Perhaps your attitude and moods lately are a bit much for them, Dante. They're kids, not little robots. They can tell when their father is not up to his usual self, and they don't want any part of it. Can't blame them, really."

"No shit."

Catrina sucked air through her teeth in a hiss, and her gaze darkened. "That's your response to what I just said?"

Dante side-eyed the stove, and noticed the red light and timer. "Are you cooking something? It smells good in here."

Catrina stood from her chair, and tipped her head to the side. She pointed a single red-tipped stiletto fingernail at her husband with a nod, like she just had some bright idea. As though she knew exactly what he was up to.

"What happened today, *bello*?"

"The usual fucking shit," Dante muttered.

"And you're pissed."

"Of course. It's a regular thing for me now, isn't it?"

Catrina came closer, and so did her pointed finger. "So you thought to come home and pick a fight with me, is that it?"

Dante blinked.

His wife stood her ground.

"You need an outlet," Catrina added, "and it's *me*."

"Can't be the kids. Can't be people at work. Can't be useless fucking made men who don't *listen*."

"So it has to be your wife."

Dante lifted a single brow. "You're the only one who might be able to fight or fuck this mood out of me, Cat."

His wife smirked a bit.

"The kids are with Antony, by the way. He took them to see the parade."

Great.

Yet another thing he missed out on this year.

"Can we yell a little before we start?" he asked.

Catrina shrugged. "As long as I get to go first."

He didn't mind that a bit.

December 10ᵗʰ

Catrina laughed breathlessly—a bitter ring clinging to her amusement—as she found herself flipped over, and pushed to the edge of the bed. Her laughter only spurred her husband on more, urging his baser needs to come out and play.

She didn't mind that at all.

Dante bent her over the bed, slapped her ass hard enough to take her breath away, and then he was kicking her legs apart again. He gave no warning before he split her open with his cock once more—the thrust sending her up on her toes and crying out as bliss saturated her senses.

At least when he was fucking her, he was focusing on something other than his problems. Or rather, he was focusing that anger into something worth doing.

Every brutal thrust brought Catrina closer and closer to the edge. Dante had been playing the tease game for a while, now, denying her orgasm whenever it came close enough that she could practically taste it.

His hands fisted her hair, yanked her back, and he fucked her harder.

Damn, she was wet.

Slick down her inner thighs.

Sweat beading on her spine.

Shaky in her knees.

"Fuck, fuck, fuck," Catrina chanted.

Dante's husky laughter practically skipped across her skin. He pounded harder into her from behind, and fireworks lit like sparks over her skin.

"Like that, *amore*? That's what you wanted, wasn't it?"

"You're such an asshole, *bello*."

Her insult only made his tempo increase. One of his hands left her hair to wrap around her throat. His fingers tightened just enough to make her see stars.

She thought to insult him again, if only to see what else she could get out of it, but she didn't. Instead, she gave into the cloyingly sweet release bubbling up through her gut and spilling into her bloodstream.

Don't fucking stop.

It became her mantra as the orgasm raced through her body.

Catrina damn near sobbed her way through the force of it. So damn intense, like nothing else. They weren't a big fight and fuck couple. It encouraged couples to fight more often just to fuck, so they could feel that way again.

Sometimes, though, it was worth it.

Like now.

"Jesus Christ," Dante grunted behind her. And then louder, "Fuck, Cat."

She felt him pull out a second before warm cum painted her naked back. He didn't let go of the hold he had on her body, or her hair, as he rubbed his dick through the semen, smearing it across her overheated skin.

Catrina used the few seconds she had to catch her breath. It didn't really help.

This had started with a few shouts.

Then, Catrina had got in Dante's face. Something she *never* did. Catrina was not the kind of woman who needed to get up close and personal in a man's space to get him riled up. She could do that from twenty feet away, fully dressed, and with a fucking smile on her face.

She wanted to *push*, Dante, though.

She had to.

And what did her husband do?

He laughed her.

Fucking laughed.

Catrina might have slapped him, but she couldn't say. What came after that was a blur of biting kisses, stinging words, and then the *bed*.

Them, and the bed.

Dante's husky chuckles rang out from behind Catrina. "You going to roll over, or what?"

"And make a mess on the bed?"

"Fuck that."

Dante flipped her over before Catrina could argue further. Her husband leaned down over her, and placed a much softer kiss to her lips than he had given her earlier. She bet there were still teeth marks inside her lip from his bite.

"I will help you change the bedding," he murmured against her lips.

Catrina swallowed the lump forming in her throat, and nodded. "All right."

"You good?"

Sore in all the right places.

Suddenly tired like never before.

Blissed.

"Happily fucked," she told him.

Dante grinned. "Same."

Catrina reached up and placed her palm against Dante's cheek. Beneath her hand, she could still feel the tic working there. A sure sign of his stress and irritation. At least he wasn't physically showing it more than that, though.

"The kids will be back soon," she told him.

He cleared his throat, and looked away. "I'll ... take them out for a movie."

Worked for her.

It would give Catrina the chance to figure something else out for him. This had not been enough. That much was clear.

"I love you, *bello*."

Dante smiled, turned his head into her hand, and kissed her palm. "I know, Cat. Too much, I think."

Never.

She didn't correct him.

• • •

Catrina sat on the edge of the desk both she and her husband used, and placed the ringing phone to her ear. After only a couple of rings, her mother-in-law picked up the call.

"Cecelia," Catrina said, smiling. "I expected Antony."

She had called his office phone number, after all.

Cecelia laughed. "The kids tired him out today. He's dead to the world in bed at the moment. We won't tell him that I let you in on the secret, though."

"Never."

All men had their things.

Antony's was refusing to acknowledge that he was getting older, and couldn't always do what he had once done as a younger man.

The rest of them, however, said nothing.

"What can I do for you?" Cecelia asked. "Is this about the party details from yesterday? I know it's a bit much and on a short deadline, but I'm sure you girls can handle it."

Catrina waved those worries away with a quick, "It's not the party, don't concern yourself over that, Cecelia."

"Then what?"

"Dante."

"Dante," her mother-in-law echoed.

Catrina called Antony because she thought her husband's father might have a perspective on his son that could help her. One that might point her in the right direction where handling Dante's stress and moods became a bit easier on them all.

Now, with Cecelia on the line, Catrina had a different thought. Her mother-in-law might be the better person to ask for perspective. Cecelia, too, had married a boss and lived with him through the most difficult times. She had to know what to do—or give Catrina some kind of worthy, usable advice.

"Did Antony ever have … spells of bad moods?" Catrina asked. Before Cecelia could answer, she added, "You know, times when work and life and all the rest got to be too much, and he didn't handle it well. When nothing you did helped."

After a long pause, Cecelia replied, "Usually every few years or so."

"Like clockwork?"

"Men like Antony don't know how to … well, relax, I guess. Just taking vacations for him were not actually vacations. Business was almost always involved somehow. So yes, I would say he didn't know how to properly relax. It was something he needed to learn over time."

"Did you help him with that?"

"Sometimes, and other times, I just let him work it out on his own."

"Well, that is not going to work here," Catrina muttered.

"Ah," her mother-in-law said. "I'm assuming the time of year isn't helping Dante, either."

"Likely not."

"There isn't much I can do to help, Cat, except to say that regardless, it will pass. In the meantime, force him to take a step back, and relax."

"I don't know how to do that."

Cecelia hummed on the other end of the line. "I know someone who does."

December 11th

Dante didn't look up from the work spread out on his desk as someone entered his office. No one got inside his office at Empire Developments unless their name was on the list, or they were an investor that put a lot of zeroes behind their name.

Basically, important people.

"Son."

Antony was one of the important people.

Still, Dante didn't look up. "Dad."

"You busy, son?"

"A little. I have something coming up that I need to

approve."

"Looks like a new build to me," Antony said as he came closer.

Dante leaned back just enough to let his father look over a few of the plans and proposed contracts for a new fifty floor building Empire Developments wanted to nab in upper Manhattan. A condo build for expensive clients. Apparently, already half of the condos were bought *with* contracts signed even though the building wasn't up yet. Dante wanted to be the company that put forth the right number to get that contract.

"You're never going to step back from this company and relax a bit, are you?" his father asked.

"Nope. I guess you shouldn't have fired me from Marcello Industries all those years ago. Look at what you could have had, Papa."

Antony chuckled. "Ouch, Dante."

He eyed his father, and shrugged a shoulder. "I was joking."

"I know."

Antony quieted as he gazed around Dante's office. He didn't need to follow his father's stare to know what the man was seeing. Glass walls that served as floor to ceiling windows and overlooked New York City. A city that was currently being blanketed in falling white snowflakes. Across the office, the two walls separating Dante from the rest of the floor were currently frosted for privacy, but could be cleared with a push of a button.

"Do you realize I have never been in your office before?"

Dante looked up at that statement. "No, I didn't really think about it. I guess you haven't been up this far. Usually, you're waiting in the lobby if you drop by."

Antony smiled. "Maybe I didn't want to step on your toes, son."

"Marcello Industries sold years ago, Papa. You couldn't possibly step on my toes."

"First, it's now called Crevier Industries, and—"

"I know, I regularly go against them in bidding wars. I also regularly win. Stupid name for that company."

Antony snorted. "I thought so, too, but in the contracts for the sale was that they were required to change the name."

Dante leaned back in his chair. His attention was finally caught enough that he felt safe to let the work on his desk linger for a while without him. Besides, he had just learned something very interesting.

"You never told me that," Dante said. "I just assumed they changed their name because they didn't want to be associated with what the Marcello name means here in New York."

"If anything, keeping the name might have given them an edge."

"Well … true."

"I didn't want *our* name attached to a company we no longer had a hand in, son."

Huh.

"And *secondly*," Antony added before Dante could say something else, "by not wanting to step on your toes, I meant that I never wanted you to feel like imposing my presence here was intended to change how you did business as the CEO of this company, Dante."

"I never would have felt like that."

Antony shook a finger at him and smiled. "I think you would have, but now, we will never have to worry about it. See what I did there?"

Dante laughed, and went back to surveying the work on his desk. "So what brought you over to my side of town today, anyway?"

"Catrina, actually."

"What, is she not doing what Ma wants her to do for that Christmas party, or something?"

"I assume Catrina is doing just fine. I think Cecelia even mentioned Catrina was handling the catering side of things, and whatnot."

"She's already cooked some stuff, too. Froze it so it would be good."

And nearly broke Dante's knuckles with a wooden spoon when he tried to steal some of the sweets. Fuck his life …

"No, I came here because she called about you, son," Antony said.

Dante's head popped right back up again. "I beg your pardon?"

"Your wife."

"Yeah, I got that."

Antony nodded. "She called about *you*."

Dante tried all he could not to show the irritation suddenly boiling inside his bloodstream, and failed miserably. All his father did was raise an eyebrow while Dante grinded his fucking teeth.

"Oh she did, huh?"

"Technically, your mother," Antony said, "but it was meant for me. Cecelia passed the information along. You've been in some kind of mood for quite a while. I think Catrina assumed it was passing the rest of us by, but we have all gotten a taste of your attitude over these past couple of months."

His father waved a hand high in the air, adding, "According to your wife, it's gotten progressively worse.

You're not handling … well, whatever it is that's bothering you very well. Stress, I assume. Work, likely. Cosa Nostra. It all piles and piles and piles, doesn't it? Before we realize what's even happening, it's already happened."

Dante just kept grinding his teeth while his father talked. Mostly, he was pissed the fuck off that his wife thought it would be okay to go to his parents about the fact he was having issues. They kept their private business private for a *reason*.

This was one of those things.

"Dad, it's not your concern," Dante told him. "Now, if you'll excuse me, I have some work to do, and I really need to get it done."

"Could you say that with less bite in your tone?"

"Not at the moment."

"You're angry."

"Wouldn't you be in my situation?" Dante asked. "I handle my business just fine on my own. I do not need anyone else getting into it. I will be sure to pass that little message along to my wife when I get home. Apparently, she needs a reminder."

"Or she cares about you and is concerned. Have you thought of taking a break?"

Dante scoffed.

Hard, loud, and rude.

He pushed away from his work and desk, sitting straight and staring his father head-on. Antony didn't bat an eye at Dante's anger resurfacing.

"A break, really? I have too much work between this fucking place and *la famiglia* to even consider taking a break. That's before I even get into mentioning my wife and kids, or the time of year. Oh, and let's not forget that I am still waiting on Gio to at least get me *some* good news on the Lucian front, so I know if he's going to be out of jail before Christmas gets here."

Antony brushed off invisible lint from his suit. "And what if I could provide all of that for you, son? Someone to handle *famiglia* business. Someone to be here. Your children. Lucian. All of it. What if it was all handled? Would you take a short break and get back to a place where you can recharge?"

"Well, then, you'd have to be fucking Santa Claus, Papa."

Antony grinned.

It looked like a challenge.

"Ho, ho, ho, Dante."

December 15th

Catrina barely got the big front doors to the Marcello mansion opened before her kids pushed in front of her to dart inside their grandparents' home. They almost knocked her right off her feet in their rush. Their laughter lit up the halls and echoed back. Cecelia was likely cooking something sweet because the scent of confection sugar clung heavily in the air.

"Grandpapa!" Michel shouted, heading for the stairs.

"Grandmamma, I'm here!" Catherine called, following a different path than her brother toward the kitchen.

Neither one of the two kids had even thought to take off their jackets, mitts and hat, or their snowy boots. They didn't even look back at their mother who struggled with a small duffle bag for each of them.

Catrina didn't really mind, though. She knew the two were excited to spend a few days with their grandparents. Plus, she might have mentioned that a little time away would do their daddy wonders. Not time away from them, per say, just … time.

The two seemed to understand.

Catrina set the duffle bags down on the floor in the great hall with a huff. She didn't bother to remove her own jacket or boots because she wouldn't be staying long. She was just here to drop off the kids, and move onto the next thing on her list.

Then, Dante …

Shortly after, Cecelia came out of a connecting hallway with a smile on her face. Catherine was right on her grandmother's heels.

"Is that everything?" Cecelia asked, gesturing at the bags.

"Enough for a few days."

"They have proper clothes for the Christmas party, right?"

"I have the *prettiest* dress, Grandmamma," Catherine

butted in. "It's red and white, like Ma's."

Catrina bent down to stroke her mini-me's cheek with her palm. "It is just like Ma's. I love you, *reginella*. You be good for your grandmother. I don't want to hear about you fighting with your brother or causing problems. Understand?"

Catherine nodded. "I won't, Ma."

She said that, but …

The two siblings fought like cats and dogs sometimes. Cecelia said it was normal. All siblings battled like that. Catrina hoped it was the case, and would wane as her kids got older.

Besides, even if the two did get into some kind of spat, Cecelia wouldn't say a thing to Catrina or Dante. She would handle it all on her own like she always did with the kids. It was just the woman's way.

"Come here," Catrina said, pulling Catherine close. She hugged her daughter, and kissed Catherine's forehead and little puckered lips. "Love you, my girl."

"Love you, Ma."

Standing, Catrina faced her mother-in-law. "Call me if you need something, or if they get to be too much."

Cecelia scoffed. "Please, Catrina. I raised three boys who were far rowdier than your two. This is nothing."

Mmhmm.

Catrina had no doubt.

"Everything for the party on your end is taken care of, right?" Cecelia asked.

She could tell her mother-in-law was concerned about the party details, but wasn't willing to put her hands into the pot. It was her guarantee for that year, after all.

"You don't need to worry, Cecelia. It is all taken care of. I am going from here to sign off on the final catering details for the last bit of dishes. I talked to Jordyn and Kim. They assured me that they are more than fine with handling the rest of the decorating without me. It's all going to be fantastic."

Cecelia smiled. "I have all the faith, Cat."

Catrina raised a brow. "All the faith?"

"Most of it."

Yeah.

She thought so.

• • •

Catrina stood on the front steps of Empire Developments. Snow fell down in heavy flakes as she stared up the length of the tall building to the floor where she knew her husband's office was situated. She had called Dante thirty minutes ago, and was now just about done waiting.

He did not want her going in there to get him.

Guaranteed.

Glancing over her shoulder, Catrina found the car waiting to take her and Dante away for the next few days. The driver—one of her husband's enforcers—looked as though he really wished he could get back inside the car and warm up.

Catrina turned back to the building only to see Dante *finally* exiting the front doors. He walked the thirty feet to greet her, and dropped a kiss on her cheek.

"A little early to be leaving work, isn't it?" he asked.

Catrina nodded. "For you, yes."

"Then what's this all about, *bella donna*?"

Beautiful woman.

Catrina smiled. "It's time for that break, Dante."

Her husband cocked an eyebrow. "Pardon?"

"A break. You need one. Someone helped to set this up, and make sure everything you needed covered would be handled for the next few days."

Dante eyed the waiting car. He had been so incredibly pissed at his wife for going to his parents that their silent feud over it lasted for a couple of days. While he thought the whole thing was over, and his wife forgot about the break thing, clearly she had not.

"How many days, Catrina?"

"Until the twentieth."

"The Christmas party."

She nodded.

"Technically," Catrina added, "that is when we're going to pick up the kids, and attend the party. However …"

Dante wet his lips with his tongue, and kept a sharp eye on his wife. "Keep going, Cat."

"You will not be returning to work until after the New Year."

"You know I can't do that. I have—"

Catrina waved at the car and interjected with, "Get in the vehicle, Dante."

"Catrina."

Again, she waved at the car.

Dante didn't move.

Neither did she.

"Cat, I can't just … go off for a while."

"You can and you will, Dante. This is not the time for arguments. You need a break. You need to stop and enjoy just being for a while. I have made this happen. The car is waiting. We are burning gas for nothing. Your enforcer would greatly like to warm up as you made us wait thirty unnecessary minutes while you probably yelled at someone over the phone up there."

"I did—"

Catrina's gaze narrowed.

Dante cleared his throat. "Okay, so maybe I was busy doing something of that nature. But I was *working*, Catrina. You know, doing my goddamn job."

"A job that is killing you lately, Dante."

"It's more than just this place. It's Cosa Nostra. It's missing out on my kids' Christmas things. It's not even getting to enjoy the first snowfall of the year."

"I know. And so we have done something to help with that, if you would only shut your mouth and get in that car."

Dante eyed the car again. "My apologies, *amore*."

"Get in the car, *bello*."

He did.

Without further argument.

December 18th

"I don't think you've ever looked as handsome as you do right now," Catrina said.

Dante glanced away from the Waldorf Astoria's window to see his wife standing in the entryway connecting the bedroom with the sitting room.

The very beautiful hotel room might as well have been a small apartment, considering the size. Every inch of the space dripped with expensive taste and an old money feel. Hardwood floors and priceless rugs. Antique furniture pieces and tasteful artwork. A whole wet bar full of top shelf liquor.

His kind of place.

Catrina had picked well.

"Handsome?" he asked.

Catrina leaned her hip against the doorjamb, and watched him through lowered lashes. All these years, and it only took a single look from his wife to get his heartrate picking up, and his blood heated. God, he loved her for that, too.

"That's what I said," Catrina replied.

Dante wasn't doing shit but lounging on a chaise and overlooking the busy Manhattan street outside. He wasn't even fully dressed as he hadn't bothered to finishing buttoning up the silk dress shirt he slid on earlier, or knot his tie.

"If you say so, *amore*."

Catrina flashed him a grin, and made her way across the room to him. His hand pressed into the curve of her back, and pushed her even closer so that he could rest his cheek against her thigh. She dragged long nails through his short hair, letting her fingers run over his scalp in the best fucking way.

"Ready to get back to life in a couple of days?" Catrina asked.

"Now I am, yes."

"I knew you would come around to this."

Dante grinned, and kissed her naked thigh. Like him, she hadn't fully gotten dressed either after their escapade earlier that day. She was still wearing the peach-colored silk robe that only fell to her mid-thigh. The belt cinched at the waist showed off her hourglass figure perfectly.

"It's a nice sight from up here, isn't it?" Catrina asked.

He peered back out the window.

White blanketed the streets and sidewalks in heavy sheets. Red and gold Christmas decorations hung from lampposts and overtop windows. The fast walking people were bundled up, and seemingly unbothered by the white flakes falling down from the gray-blue sky.

"They're all just … rushing," Dante said.

Catrina bent down and kissed him with one of her sly smiles. "And you're not."

"Apparently."

For the first day or so, it bugged the hell out of Dante. He wanted nothing more than to call and check up on people. Giovanni, his father, and a Capo that he had been having issues with over the last few weeks.

Plus, his business. He had left an entire contract just hanging in the fucking wind when he got inside that damn car. There was so much he had left undone, and yeah, that had pricked at every single one of his nerves.

Then, there was also his kids. He missed them like crazy, too.

Although, Catrina FaceTimed Michel and Catherine twice a day. It was the only time she allowed Dante to have a phone in his hands.

His wife was a fucking tyrant.

A beautiful one, but still.

Catrina, however, had taken his phone the very second he sat his ass down in the town car. She told him the details about where they would be staying, and a few other things she had planned for the five days they would be unreachable.

Dante walked into the hotel room to find the phone on the nightstand only connected to the kitchen, and the front desk. Catrina had been smart enough to know she needed to make sure that little detail was taken care of, too.

He had to give his wife credit, though. This was exactly what he needed, no questions asked. Time away. Space from people and life. A barrier between him and business. A few days to simply take care of his wants and needs, instead of handling every other aspect of his life except for himself.

That anger and irritation that had been constantly building inside his mind and heart for weeks was now nonexistent. The bit of time to clear his head had actually given him different outlooks on how problems could be fixed with less arguments, and on a faster timeline.

He greatly wanted to get back to his kids, as well. He wanted to enjoy the rest of the time he was going to have with them over the holidays to make memories he might have not done otherwise.

Dante needed time to stop, breathe, and recharge.

Nothing more.

His wife had given him that, or rather … helped to make it possible for him. He was so grateful. More than Catrina could possibly know.

This was *the best* Christmas gift ever.

A gift he hadn't even known he needed.

"I have something for you," Catrina said.

Dante stared up at his wife. "Oh?"

"Yep. Here."

She handed over an envelope. It wasn't properly sealed, so Dante just pulled out what looked to be a letter. Unfolding the two flaps, he instantly recognized the handwriting of his father.

Dante,

Even the best bosses occasionally need to take a break, son. Even those men who live and breathe this life have to take time to remember what it was about this thing of ours that made us hand over everything for it in the first place.

Next time, recognize your need.

And take care of it.

I thought you might like to know a few things. I'm sure—even though Catrina has told me you're enjoying your little time away—that you still have some things on your mind. They were weighing on mine, too.

The company won the bid. I sat in on it. Give your COO a raise. He deserves it. Thank him with something worth his while, Dante. Also, try to give him a little more leeway for this sort of thing. He's proved he can handle it.

Giovanni has the family and business handled. You didn't think I would let that go unmanned, did you? Thank your brother. When it is his time to take a break, you will allow him to have it and do so with a smile.

Lucian will be out tomorrow, probably around the evening. He will be at the Christmas party, and his kids will have him home.

Once again, thank your brother for that, too.

Oh, and me. You can thank me—and your wife—for this time away. You needed it, but we won't always be able to hand it to you, Dante. You have to learn to do it for yourself.

Merry Christmas, son, and never underestimate the power of this Santa.

Ho, ho, ho.

Dante laughed as he folded the letter back up. He

swore he could hear his father's smugness coming through each and every word he had written.

Catrina stroked his cheek. "Good news?"

"Very good, Cat."

"*Ti amo, bello.*"

Dante pulled his wife down to his lap, tipped her back, and kissed her. "*Ti amo, mia cara bella.*"

December 20th

Catrina put the finishing touch on Catherine's hair with a red bow that matched her red and white dress. Catherine tipped her head back to stare up at her mother with a toothy smile that made Catrina's heart melt.

It was like looking into a younger mirror when she stared at Catherine. They shared the same delicate features and smile. Even the way her daughter cocked her eyebrow when someone said something she didn't like was just the same as Catrina.

Those greens eyes and that dark hair was all Dante, though.

"Do I look pretty, Ma?" Catherine asked.

Catrina kissed the tip of her girl's nose. "The *most* pretty, Catherine."

"I look like you. We match."

Well, mostly.

Catrina's dress was a tighter fit, and sexier. Adult to Catherine's sweet child dress. They were the same satin, though, and the same red with white accents. Even the red kitten heels Catherine wore were similar to her mother's sky-high Prada stilettos.

"We do," Catrina said.

Catherine preened.

"Let's go show Daddy, huh?"

She helped her daughter down from the large bed. They had used one of the many guest bedrooms in the Marcello mansion to ready for the Christmas party, while Dante and Michel had opted to use her husband's old bedroom.

The kids had practically crawled up their father's legs the second he walked into the mansion. They didn't let go of him for a couple of hours after, either.

Catrina had planned for that, though. She made sure they got there in lots of time for the kids to reunite with them after their five days away, plus prep for the guests that would be soon arriving to party.

She reminded herself once again to thank her sisters-in-law for pulling extra weight with the whole party thing. She should have been here to help decorate more, and set up.

Kim and Jordyn got it, though.

Everyone needed a moment to breathe.

Catherine held tight to her mother's hand as they headed down the long hallway to where Dante was readying himself and Michel. Sweet as could be, Catherine skipped along at Catrina's side with a wide smile.

Every step her daughter took made her dress swing back and forth with a swishing sound. Catherine put a little extra bounce in her step just to make it that much louder.

Catrina couldn't help but laugh.

"I was a good girl for Grandmamma and Grandpapa," Catherine told her mother.

Outside the bedroom door, Catrina brushed a stray curl off her daughter's shoulder. "I knew you would be."

Catrina knocked twice on the bedroom door, and waited for her husband to call her inside.

"It's open."

Inside, Catrina found Dante was finishing with Michel by showing him how to knot his tie properly in the mirror.

"And then we pull it just like this," Dante said.

Catrina smiled.

Michel, too, matched his father in a black suit with a matching red vest and tie. The two looked as handsome as could be.

"Thanks, Dad."

Dante patted Michel on the very top of his head. "You got it, son."

"Looks at me, Daddy!"

Catherine did a little twirl. Dante's laughter lit up the room as he came to bend down in front of Catherine. He flipped out the skirt of her dress, and made sure the buckles on her shoes were snapped well. Then, he straightened her bow a bit.

"My pretty *bambina*," he told her.

Catherine preened all over again.

She liked her compliments, as far as that went.

"You have to make sure you don't get dirty, right?" Dante asked.

"I don't *like* dirt, Daddy."

Catrina snorted.

Dante nodded. "I know, Catherine."

"Michel, why don't you take your sister down to see Grandmamma and Grandpapa?" Catrina asked.

"Sure, Ma."

Michel snagged his sister's outstretched hand before

the two darted from the room. That left Catrina and Dante all alone.

Dante stood, and allowed Catrina to check him over. She went over his suit with her hands, brushing away invisible lint that didn't exist. She pretended to check his red tie and matching napkin, but those were perfectly knotted and folded as well.

Nothing new.

"You look beautiful," Dante murmured.

Catrina smiled. "Oh?"

"The *most* beautiful."

She laughed. "I am not like Catherine, *bello.* Compliments don't do much for me, you know."

"I still like to tell you."

"I still like it when you do, too."

Dante grinned a sexy sight. "I know. Do you want to do a little twirl for me, too? Let me see what those heels do for your legs?"

"You know exactly what they do for my legs, and better yet, what they do when they're wrapped around your head."

"Damn, *donna.*"

Catrina flashed her teeth and winked. "Save that for later. After all, you have a while before you have to worry about anything other than making me happy, and entertaining our kids."

"True."

"I expect breakfast in bed tomorrow," Catrina told him.

Dante nodded. "Done."

"And you can help me out of this dress later."

"The heels stay on, though."

"Of course."

• • •

"Papa."

Antony smiled wide as he approached Dante and Catrina. "Son. Don't you look … *happy*."

"That's as good of a word as any," Dante replied.

The Christmas party was in full swing. All the guests had arrived with no problems. The first course of food had been served. Bubbly champagne and red wine was being passed around. Santa had come for all the little ones in the mansion.

Lucian had finally made his appearance to surprise his wife and kids. Although, Catrina didn't know where Jordyn and Lucian had disappeared to for the moment.

Cecelia was fully enjoying herself, proud of the way the girls handled the party, *and* didn't have a bad word to say about anything.

Catrina counted all of that as a battle won for herself.

And her sisters-in-law.

"Where is Catherine and Michel?" Antony asked.

"Likely trying to get a second go at Santa," Catrina replied.

Dante chuckled. "They were convinced he wouldn't recognize who they were a second time around what with all the kids."

"You tried that once, too," Antony said.

"Really?"

Antony nodded. "Didn't realize I was the one in the suit, though. You were about three, or so."

"Classic Dante," Catrina said.

Her husband patted her on the ass, although not in an obvious fashion.

"Your mother would like a dance," Antony told Dante.

Catrina's husband looked to her.

She shrugged.

"I guess I'll take Antony, then."

Antony, in his Santa hat and with a wide smile, offered his arm. "It's not a second pick, Catrina. Who do you think taught that husband of yours to dance?"

"My mother," Dante said over his shoulder.

"And me, thank you," Antony replied.

"Yes, thank you," Catrina said. "For everything, Antony."

The Marcellos were a lot of things …

The very best family was right at the top of the list.

Antony's smile softened. "Someone wanted the best Christmas for everyone this year, Catrina. I was only giving her what she wanted."

Catrina didn't ask who her father-in-law meant. She didn't need to.

He clearly meant his own wife.

Antony was every single reason why his sons loved their wives the way they did.

Entirely. Wholly. Fully.

Unwavering. Always.

The kind of love that scared people. The kind of love that never failed.

So yeah, for that, Catrina would forever be grateful.

Giovanni & Kim

December 10ᵗʰ

"Are you listening to me?"

Kim rolled her eyes upward at her husband's question. "Of course I'm listening to you, Giovanni."

"Really, because I asked you the same question three times. You didn't answer."

Under her breath, Kim cursed at having been caught. Across the room, her six-year-old son, Andino, watched the National Geographic Channel.

"Bad word," Andino said.

He didn't even turn around.

Little tattletale.

"Sorry, Gio," Kim grumbled.

"You're a little distracted."

Yep.

Not news.

"What was the question?"

"Did you pick up the stuff from the post office—Andino's gifts we ordered online?"

"Yes," Kim said. "I managed to do that."

"Is it the party stuff?"

"Pardon?"

"The party, *Tesoro*. Ma's party. Is that what's got you in a whole different world today, or what?"

"Basically," Kim admitted. "I have to handle the decorations. Jordyn's got guests, invitations, and all that junk. Catrina took over the catering, minus the stuff we decided to cook ourselves. But the decorating—"

"It's a lot," Gio interjected.

Kim nodded to herself.

A whole lot.

She had several rooms within the Marcello mansion to decorate. They were not small rooms, either. Adding onto that little issue, Cecelia had ways she did things. Kim's mother-in-law preferred for everything to be as real as possible.

So sure, while they had decorations to use, a lot was going to need to be purchased, made, or brought in. It was not a simple task.

And Kim had …

Oh, ten fucking days to get it done!

"Bad word," Andino said again, still not turning away from the television.

"Did I say all that out loud?" Kim asked.

Gio's chuckles echoed through the phone. "Yeah, you did."

"Great."

Kim massaged at her temples, and willed the oncoming headache away. She knew it wouldn't do her any good. The damn thing was going to be her constant companion and unwanted best friend until she figured all this shit out.

"Kim, you're freaking out over nothing," Gio assured.

"Oh, really?"

"Yeah, really."

"Okay, so you get your ass home and come handle these tasks for me, Gio."

"Can't."

"Because you don't *want* to," she grumbled.

"No, because I don't have time, *Tesoro*."

Kim checked her attitude. She knew that her husband was telling the truth. And besides, if Gio could help her, he would. He was great that way. Unfortunately, Gio had a whole bunch of his own shit he needed to handle.

A brother in lockup. Another brother—also his *boss*—that just seemed to be having a bad month. Business for his *famiglia* and as Dante's consigliere. Christmas for them, and making sure his parents had a good holiday, too.

Their son …

Speaking of Andino.

"I want the whales, Ma," Andino said, finally looking over his shoulder at her. "See, those kinds, Ma. I want them for Christmas."

Kim eyed the damn documentary playing on the television. Unsurprisingly, killer whales slipped through the water alongside a large boat that was filming them. It was Andino's new thing—killer whales, that was. At some point, he had watched or read something at school, came home, and was obsessed.

"Can I put it on my list, Ma?" Andino asked.

Kim pursed her lips, unsure how to explain to their child that, no, a whale could not be brought into their house. Andino wasn't going to take no for an answer. He was too smart for his own good, and would ask a million and one questions that would absolutely make sense, but

lonely in the corner."

"You gotta put Andino's gifts somewhere, right?"

"Cute, smartass."

"Call them, *Tesoro*. Almost half of your decorating issues will be done, and Ma will be satisfied because it'll be real."

God, she loved her husband.

"Thanks," she said.

Kim swore she could feel Gio's smile when he said, "It's what I do, babe."

Mmhmm.

He did a whole hell of a lot, really. No one ever really pointed it out, or thanked Gio properly, but her husband stepped up when it came to his family. He took care of everybody, without question. He got shit done for them.

"I wonder if I could hire someone to decorate the rest," Kim said.

Gio laughed darkly. "Kim, don't get too many bright ideas like that. You know how Ma is; you have to do the majority on your own."

"Burst my bubble why don't you."

"I'm not Willy Wonka."

Kim snorted. "And you don't sugarcoat shit."

"Nope."

"Bad word," Andino said again from his spot in front

of the television.

Kim shook her head. "Okay, Gio, you really need to have a talk with that kid about being a tattletale."

"Put it on the list, Kim. Put it on the list."

Their lists just kept growing …

December 13th

Giovanni Marcello typically liked when Christmas rolled around. It was the only time of the year when everyone settled a bit, relaxed, and had some fun. He was always up for fun.

This year, however, was proving to be very different.

He balanced the cell phone between his shoulder and ear as he unlocked the front door to his Amityville home. Before he even picked up his father's call, he knew Antony was about to shove something else into his lap.

It had been one thing after another this year.

"Get to the point, Papa," Gio said.

Antony grumbled a warning under his breath and a quick, "Should have just waited until the morning to call you."

"That would have been appreciated."

It was closing in on eleven at night. Gio had been from one end of New York City to the other from morning until evening. Life did not seem to want to slow down for him at the moment, and he really needed a few spare minutes to breathe.

Or to spend loving his wife.

To talk to his son.

Something.

Stepping inside his house, the first thing he noticed was that the lights were off and the place was quiet. Gio cursed internally, knowing Kim had likely run around like a chicken with her head cut off all day between Andino and planning that goddamn Christmas party.

He had meant to get home earlier and help her with their son—Andino wasn't always a handful, but he certainly liked attention—but shit came up. Something was always fucking coming up lately.

At least with the lights off and the house quiet, he could safely assume Kim had managed to wrangle their kid into bed. Hopefully, without much trouble.

"I would like for you to handle Dante's

responsibilities until after the New Year rolls around," Antony finally said.

Gio kicked his Italian loafers into a corner. "Seriously?"

"*He's* not going to admit he needs a break. He's been in a mood for a good month. Now, he's snapping at everybody, and it's … Well, Jesus, he needs to relax."

"We all need to relax!"

"You know how hard your brother works, Gio," Antony said quietly.

Okay, that was true enough. As the boss of the Marcello Cosa Nostra, Dante's plate was constantly overflowing with business to handle. As was Gio's, as his older brother's consigliere. Not to mention Lucian's, as the family's underboss. They were all busy—minus Lucian, but Gio gave him a break considering his current state.

"His mood has been worsening," Antony pointed out.

Well, that was true, too.

Gio couldn't deny it.

Fuck.

Gio shrugged off his jacket, and hung it on a waiting hook. "Well, yeah, but that doesn't change what I said, either."

"Listen, it's the holidays, son. Dante keeps me

informed, so I know what's happening. His tribute for the month is already done. The Capos are quiet with Christmas coming up. There's not a lot of business going on. He has a meeting coming up with the Donati boss—Calisto—for something or other. It'll be easy. The guys will just defer to you."

"*Dad.*"

"What?"

"They're already deferring to me," Gio said with a heavy sigh. "Because of Lucian being in fucking lockup."

"You don't need to swear."

"I kind of feel like I do."

Antony muttered something too low for Gio to understand before adding louder, "I'm asking you to do this for your brother."

"Adding onto all the stuff I already am doing," Gio replied. "My family, all the shit for the holidays, *and* working to get Lucian out of jail in time for Christmas. You're killing me here, Dad. Give me a break, please."

"One man at a time, Gio. You will get yours."

Gio scowled at the mirror showcasing his frustrated expression. "I better."

Antony chuckled. "All in due time. So you will handle this for Dante, then?"

"Did he put you up to this?"

"No," Antony admitted.

Gio cocked a brow. "Have you even told him?"

"He's not going to realize how much he needs this until it's given. Call it a gift. I don't give a damn, honestly."

"Yeah, well, you know Dante."

"I do," Antony grumbled.

"So good luck with that, Papa."

"Mmm. Good night, Gio."

"Night."

Gio hung up the call, and tried to ignore the suddenly overwhelming sensation of heaviness that came to rest upon his shoulders. Years ago, he didn't mind telling people no. He had been pretty damn good at it, actually.

Now, not so much.

Especially not when it came to his family.

Gio found his wife sleeping on the couch in the living room. Kim didn't even stir as he leaned over the back of the couch to peer down at her. He stroked her cheekbone with two fingers, happy and still for a moment. He almost wanted to wake her up, but decided better of it because she too had a lot on her plate.

Besides, his wife knew …

She always knew how Gio was with family, life, and everything else. A little more piled on wasn't going to be very much of a surprise to her.

A live Christmas tree stood in the corner of the living room. The tip nearly grazed the ten foot high ceiling. Spread around the bare tree were opened boxes of decorations. Considering the few scattered ornaments on the coffee table, Gio figured his wife had probably fallen asleep in an attempt to decorate the massive thing.

He decided to help.

He had a few minutes, after all.

Gio went about unpacking the gold and red decorations. Kim tended to favor those colors, he learned. Every Christmas, their home was a gold and red Christmasland. The only green that was ever found was on the tree, garlands, and wreath on the front door.

He wasn't sure how much time had passed as he put the finishing golden bows around the branches just the way he knew Kim liked, but he thought a couple of hours. Plugging in the cord for the white lights, the tree lit up from bottom to top.

At the tip, a golden star blinked slowly.

He then started packing up the empty boxes. At least then, Kim wouldn't wake up to another mess to clean. Her final decorating—their tree—was done, and she could mark that off her list. She didn't need to be picking up after this mess, too.

It was only then that Gio noticed the scrap of paper

on the coffee table as well. He instantly recognized the messy, child-like writing as his son's. Andino wasn't a very good speller, but he was confident. He sounded out words, and got them pretty close to how they should be spelled, for the most part. He was ahead of his class in that regard.

Gio read down the paper.

Dear Santa, it started.

A couple of remote control trucks. A book his son wanted. Something for Johnathan—Andino's cousin, Lucian's son, and his boy's best friend. It amused Gio to no end that Andino had thought to ask *Santa* for something for Johnathan.

His dad wud be good, Andino had written next to it.

Then, at the end, Andino had put, *And a whale, please. Seawurd has dem.*

He was pretty sure his son had meant to write *SeaWorld*. Gio laughed, but it quickly died. He was not going to be able to get his son a whale, or even a viewing of one. Those attractions were long closed because it was practically torture to the animals being in captivity like that.

How could he explain that to his kid, though?

Gio's countdown was on.

Twelve days to figure something out for Andino that would satisfy his newest obsession.

Add that to my list.

Chapter 21

December 14th

Kim traced the colorful tattoos spread across her husband's chest with the tips of her fingers. His muscles flexed and jumped under her touch, which only made her repeat the same soft strokes.

Already seated in Giovanni's naked lap—*on* his hard cock—she was more than happy to just … be. At least for the moment. Them, a dimly lit bedroom, quiet breaths, and fast love. Yeah, she liked that a lot.

Sometimes, this had to wait.

Other things got in the way.

That was life.

"Are you going to fuck me, or what?" Gio asked.

Kim grinned. "Patience, Gio."

"I don't want to be patient. I want to *come*."

Her laughter chimed in the bedroom. The sound quickly melted into a low moan when Gio's hands grabbed tighter to her waist. His fingers dug into her skin with just enough pressure to make her breath catch in her throat.

Gio smirked as he used his hold to pull her harder onto his cock while he flexed his hips upward at the same time. She was already soaked—already full of him and needy. She was ready. She still felt his dick jerk inside her. His movement caused her inner muscles to clench around his length in the best way.

"We should *talk* for a minute," she told him.

Gio shook his head. "Nope."

"Nope?"

"Nope."

"Gio, I woke you up early to talk."

"Lies," he said, leaning forward to nip on her bottom lip. The way his teeth cut into sensitive flesh, tugged, and stung. It felt damn good, too. His teeth in her lip, his fingers on her sides, and his cock balls-deep in her pussy. So freaking good. "You lie, Kim. You can't wake me up naked, crawling on top of me like a kitten, and then say you want to *talk*. Lies."

He was right.

Mostly.

Kim let him have that battle as a win.

Frankly, she didn't really mind. This was a win for her, too, she thought. How could it be a loss? Certainly not when it meant riding her husband to the best high life had ever given them. Sex was like their drug. It had always been that way.

Sometimes, life made them abstain. It forced them apart because business was busy, family was overwhelming, and everything else got in the way. They became two people working, getting an hour here or there where they had to choose what they did together wisely. Exhausting days, and short nights, leaving them both waking up at different times because responsibilities and priorities.

Yeah, that was their life.

And then they got *this*.

Perfect, quiet, beautiful moments like this.

"Come on, *Tesoro*, you're killing me here," Gio murmured along the column of her throat. His back rested against the suede headboard of the bed. Her wandering hands had finally come to rest along the railroad path of his flexing abs. "We fuck, then we talk. How's that?"

Kim kissed his smirking lips before he pulled back to

stare at her. "Deal."

His warm hands cupped her cheeks as he drew her in for a lingering, burning kiss that stole her breath away all over again. She didn't mind being on top doing the work for them, not when it meant she got to watch the way Gio's gaze darkened, how he flashed his teeth the faster she rode him, or when she got to hear her name coming out of his mouth.

It was usually him.

Him pounding into her.

Him making her beg.

Him demanding, promising, and *wanting*.

He still did all of that now, too, only in different ways. She liked that a lot.

Gio palmed Kim's ass as her tempo picked up. He yanked her down onto his length harder with every lift and lower of her hips. He pushed away from the headboard just enough to make their bodies tuck tightly together.

She was soft curves and sweet cries.

He was hard lines and dirty words.

They were kind of perfect that way.

"Fuck, I love your pussy first thing in the morning, Kim," he breathed in her ear. "Ride that cock for me, *Tesoro*. Give me what I want."

Almost, almost, almost …

A single, firm slap to her ass had her control splitting in two. Just like that, the orgasm raced through her nervous system while her husband chuckled darkly in her ear.

"You get so damn tight when you come—makes it hard to breathe, Kim."

While bliss of the orgasm continued washing over her senses, Kim leaned back. She put her hands to Gio's thighs and used that as a support to keep her steady. He wouldn't be long now that she had come, not when breakfast was waiting to be cooked, a kid had to get ready for school, and business was waiting to be done.

Sometimes, fast and dirty was needed.

Slow and sweet could wait.

Kim let Gio take over from there. She was more than happy to simply ride out the aftershocks of her bliss while he chased his own. Through lowered lashes, she enjoyed the sight of her husband using his strength to move her body the way he wanted. She loved seeing his muscles flex, and his gaze take in the sight of her like he was a parched man and she was his only drink.

Really, Kim just loved the way Gio loved her.

"Fuck," Gio grunted.

His exclamation was followed by three hard, sharp thrusts that damn near ached from the force. He held her tight to his cock on the last one, and she felt him finally release as deep as he could get inside her pussy.

Instantly, his arms were wrapping her tight. She buried her face along the curve where his neck met his shoulder. Gio dotted kisses along whatever spots he could reach while his fingers drifted through the loose waves of her hair.

Kim wasn't sure how long they stayed like that, but as long as the alarm clock didn't go off, and nobody knocked on their bedroom door, she didn't care. She got lost in the sensation of her husband's fingers drifting through her hair and over her skin. All the while, she watched the white tufts of snow drift down from the sky through the slightly opened shades on the bedroom window.

It made a pretty sight.

Relaxing.

Calming.

"Thank you for carrying me to bed last night," she whispered.

Gio smiled against the top of her head. "You looked tired."

"And I saw the tree."

"So you didn't wake me up first."

She laughed. "No, I went downstairs to grab my phone."

"Hmm. Is the tree good?"

"It's perfect, Gio."

Silence stretched on between them, but Kim didn't mind. She became dazed again between watching the falling snow, and enjoying the closeness of Gio.

"Maybe a stuffy thing would suffice," Gio said, breaking their silence.

Kim didn't even need to ask what he was talking about. "Andino isn't stupid, Gio. He's not going to be happy with a stuffed whale or something."

"Yeah, I know. It might soften the blow of disappointment, though."

Pushing up to sit straight once more, Kim shook her head and kissed Gio's lips. "He's going to be happy no matter what because *you* got him something."

"Even if it's not what he asks for?"

"Gio, he'd be happy if you sat on the couch all day with him and watched something about whales. Seriously."

"I know, I just—"

"Don't stress."

Gio gave her a look, but said nothing.

Kim didn't need him to.

Easier said than done.

December 16th

Giovanni helped the three bundled up kids out of the back of his SUV. Well, two. Michel was old enough to unbuckle himself and climb out.

As for Andino and Catherine, Gio helped the two littler ones out of their five-point-harness safety seats, slipped their winter coats back on, and looked them all over.

"Everybody got mittens?" he asked.

Six hands shot up. All wore mittens.

"Hats?"

Each kid pointed to the hat on their head.

They all wore snow pants, thick jackets, and scarfs, too. Ready to get in the first good snowfall of the year that finally stuck to the ground, and have some fun.

Really, Gio had to do that meeting with the Donati Cosa Nostra boss. It was supposed to be Dante's meeting, but given his brother was now enjoying time away—yet still close enough—for a break, Gio had taken it on.

And the man's kids for the day.

Antony and Cecelia were looking after Michel and Catherine otherwise.

"Give me the rules," Gio said.

"No leaving the park," Andino said.

"No talking to big people," Catherine chimed in.

"No playing in the parking lot," Michel added.

Good enough.

Gio pointed at a park bench that looked like someone had wiped the snow from it earlier. "See that there? I'll be over there with my friend. I will be watching. Don't break the rules, or we'll be leaving early. Got it?"

Three heads bobbed up and down.

"Get playing," Gio said.

With a flick of his gloved-covered hands, the three kids scattered. He tightened his fleece-lined leather jacket to keep out the chill in the air, and headed for the park bench. A good foot of snow had fallen over the night, adding onto the half a foot that had come down the day before. It blanketed everything in thick, pristine white.

Gio quite enjoyed the sight.

Across the park, Michel had climbed to the top of the snow-covered slide. Andino was working his way up as well. Catherine sat at the bottom by herself. He wasn't sure if the three were planning on playing *Who's the King of the Mountain* or what, but he silently willed them to be careful. He didn't need anyone breaking a bone or some shit.

That would not be conducive to Dante relaxing when he got a call about something like that regarding one of his kids.

Gio hadn't been sitting down on the bench for very long when a familiar black Mercedes SUV pulled into the parking lot. It was only because Gio had been friends with Calisto Donati for longer than he could remember that the Donati boss agreed to bring his son along to the park, and have their meeting there. Anyone else, and that would have been out of the question.

Just how it was.

Gio figured since he had to handle Dante's kids for the day, and do the meeting with Calisto, this would kill two birds with one stone.

Soon, Calisto headed Gio's way with his only boy in tow. Close to Andino's age, Cross Donati stood tall enough to reach his father's waist. Black curls stuck out from under the boy's wool cap.

Calisto patted Cross on the top of his head, and waved at the three kids playing across the park. "There you go, Cross. Play, huh?"

Cross made a face. "Nah."

"Seriously, you don't want to play with the kids?"

"Not really, Papa."

Calisto shot Gio a look.

Gio shrugged in response.

"Well, give me a few minutes to chat with my friend, then. Okay?"

"Okay," Cross said.

Quickly, Cross darted off to a bench close by. Calisto sat down beside Gio soon after.

"It's crazy how much he looks like you," Gio noted.

Calisto leaned back on the bench, and folded his arms over his chest. "Kills me every time he calls me his uncle in front of people."

Gio hid his frown by looking away. "I bet."

"He's getting to an age now where he doesn't give much of a shit what people think, anyway. He calls me whatever he wants—I let him."

"As you should," Gio replied.

Every man had their secrets.

Some secrets were simply more dangerous than others.

Calisto was a man with a *very* dangerous secret. Gio was one of the lucky fuckers who actually happened to know what that secret was. Cross.

To the outside world and Calisto's *famiglia*, Cross was Calisto's step-son, a child from his wife's first marriage that he had adopted on paper after he married Emma. Technically, by blood the two would be cousins, although Gio was aware that most people encouraged Cross to call Calisto his uncle.

The truth?

Cross was Calisto's biological son. The product of an affair between a boss's—a man who was now dead—wife, and Calisto.

Gio kept that secret for his friend.

He told *no one*.

Not his brothers.

Not his wife.

No one.

"Are you ever going to tell him the truth?" Gio asked before he could think better of it. He didn't really have any business asking. Calisto shot him a look. "Curious, that's all."

Calisto blew hot hair into his palms before stuffing

them into the pockets of his jacket. "Someday, maybe."

"You don't sound sure."

"I don't know *how*. At this age, he won't understand. Maybe when he's a teenager or something. Now isn't the right time. Besides, he's mine regardless. You know what I mean? I don't see what difference it would make when I love him just the same. Plus, I don't even know how I would start that conversation should I decide to tell him eventually."

"I would think to start with *I love you*, you know?"

"Someday," Calisto repeated.

"Mmm."

"I was surprised to get a call from you for this meeting."

Gio chuckled. "Somebody needed a break from life and business before he killed somebody else."

Calisto nodded. "I know that feeling. Are you looking after his kids, too, or what?"

"Just for today. Ma and Dad are looking after them until the twentieth. I'm still going to be handling the business side of things until the New Year is over, though."

"Gio, the boss," Calisto joked.

Gio groaned. "Man, I hate this job."

"You never were cut out to be a boss, I suppose."

"Never," Gio agreed vehemently.

Still, here he was.

For his brother, he kept reminding himself.

Gio and Calisto quieted as a dark-haired, green-eyed girl approached the bench where Cross was still sitting, happily alone. Catherine.

Dante's only daughter climbed up on the bench beside Cross, and the first thing she did was smile at him.

Cross smiled back.

"Did someone make a friend?" Gio asked.

Calisto snorted. "Cross? He doesn't seem to like people very much."

"There he is, man."

"I guess so."

"Business?" Gio asked, turning back to his friend.

Calisto settled into the bench once more. "Yes, let's talk business."

December 17th

Kim and Jordyn stared helplessly at one another from across the great hall inside the Marcello mansion. At this point, there wasn't much else they could do.

Between Jordyn's three kids, Andino, plus Cat and Dante's two … putting the finishing touches on the decorations for the party was going *nowhere.*

Fast.

The kids wouldn't stop moving. All six of them bounced from one end of the great hall to the other, shouting and laughing at the top of their lungs. Rarely— except for Sundays—did they get all of their kids together at the same time.

And even then, usually they had each set of parents on hand to keep some kind of control over the chaos.

"I am remembering why Lucian and I agreed to stop at three," Jordyn shouted from the other end of the hall.

Kim snorted. "Right. We all know you'll have another one someday."

"No way."

"Did either of you go make sure in a *permanent* fashion that it wouldn't happen again?"

"IUD," her sister-in-law replied.

Kim nodded. "Those still have the same fail-rate as other preventative measures, Jord."

"Yes, *including* getting a tubal or vasectomy."

Panic swelled through Kim at the thought. Her cheeks grew cold as they drained of color. Across the hall, her sister-in-law laughed. Kim realized then how fast this whole conversation had turned around on her.

"Seriously?"

This time, it was Jordyn's turn to nod empathetically at Kim. Although frankly, Kim thought Jordyn was doing it in a much more sarcastic way than she had.

"Oh, Jesus," Kim muttered to herself.

"Gio got the snip-snip done, didn't he?"

"Just ... shut your mouth, we're not talking about

fail-rates anymore."

"You brought it up, Kim."

"I am not having more kids."

Jordyn smirked and make a snipping gesture with two fingers. "Should have gotten the tubal done, too. Just in case."

"I'm still not having more kids. You, on the other hand …"

Her sister-in-law side-eyed the very noisy kiddos as they did another round of tag throughout the great hall.

Jordyn let out another little laugh. "Well, we said we were done. But hey, who the hell knows, right?"

Just what Kim figured.

She was happy with her one boy. She didn't want more kids. Catrina and Dante probably would have continued to try for more kids, but given how emotionally draining it had been just to conceive Catherine … they hadn't even mentioned trying to add a third to their team.

Lucian and Jordyn, though?

Aiming for half a baseball team.

Kim knew it.

"That'll make Antony and Cecelia happy," Kim said.

"What will make us happy?"

"Grandmamma!"

"Nana!"

Six voices echoed their love and excitement for their grandmother. Cecelia stepped into the great hall with a wide smile and opened arms. She attempted to hug all the grandchildren at once, and then ended up just giving each one their own time and attention.

Just like always.

Very little changed.

Kim passed Jordyn a look that spoke volumes without ever saying a word out loud. The scene happening a few feet away was every reason it would make her in-laws happy. Cecelia and Antony adored their grandchildren; they spoiled them, took them to give their parents breaks, and made time for each and every one of them individually.

They had been great parents.

And even greater grandparents.

Cecelia held out a bag to show the waiting kids. She was still dressed in a heavy tweed jacket, matching hat and mittens, and a pair of leather boots. "We've got popcorn, hot chocolate, and the new movie you all wanted to see. So how about you head to the—"

"Theater!" six voices shouted.

The volume nearly burst Kim's eardrums.

Twelve feet pattered against the hardwood floors as all the kids darted for the winding staircase that would lead them to the second and third level of the wing. Not a single one of the kids looked back over their shoulders as they left Kim and Jordyn behind. All they saw were their backs as they left.

Silence ensued.

Beautiful, peaceful *silence*.

Kim sighed. "Well, this is nice."

"Right?" Jordyn asked. "We should have thought of that sooner."

Cecelia smiled and winked as she shrugged off her jacket. "Sorry that took me so long, girls. Now, back to what I asked. What is this about something making Antony and me very happy?"

Jordyn shot Kim a look.

It screamed for her to lie or stay quiet.

Kim opted for a lie.

After all, it wasn't her choice to speak about someone else's choices regarding kids, having more, or not.

"I meant once we finally get all this decorating done for the Christmas party," Kim said, waving at the hall.

So far, most of the decorations were up … or rather, were sitting in the places they needed to be to be put up. The trees were all placed, including the largest one in the middle of the great hall. That's what the kids had been using to run around as they played tag.

"That will be nice," Cecelia said as she passed Kim by. "I'll keep the kids busy for an hour or two. How much do you think will be done by then?"

"Almost all," Jordyn assured.

Kim agreed.

"Good. Call for Antony if you need a hand. He can get one of the men who watch the house to come in and hang things, or ... whatever."

Cecelia waved a hand over her shoulder, and then she too was gone up the stairs. Kim and Jordyn were finally alone to do their work.

"Catrina called to let me know all the catering is set," Jordyn said.

"Oh?"

"Yep."

"How's her little break with Dante going?" Kim asked.

Jordyn smirked. "She didn't say."

"Then why do you look like something naughty just crawled up your skirt?"

"Because I assume without kids and life getting in the way, they're very much taking advantage. I would. What about you?"

A break without kids sounded heavenly.

She got what Jordyn was saying.

174

"Truth."

"Exactly." Jordyn picked up a few lines of garland, and looked them over. "Are you done with your shopping and everything else?"

Kim made a noise under her breath. "I guess."

"You don't sound sure."

"We still haven't found something for Andino yet to satisfy what he wants the most, plus Gio's been super busy because he's handling everybody else's problems instead of taking care of himself. It's just … a lot."

"I bet."

Kim wanted to get away from her problems as a conversational topic because really, they weren't issues that mattered. She was complaining for nothing, mostly.

"Cecelia's been pretty good about this whole party planning thing, hasn't she?"

Jordyn raised a brow like she was considering Kim's question. "She has. Surprising."

"Maybe. Or maybe she's ready to hand over the reins a bit in this family. Let us women handle all this stuff."

"Don't get ahead of yourself, now. You know she's going to be down here in two hours telling us to move this or that, or that something looks better somewhere else. It's Cecelia Marcello. She's like *ten* of Catrina, but you know, without the Queen Pin title and the scary knives."

"Still kind of scary, sometimes."

Even without the title and knives.

Kim laughed.

Jordyn grinned.

Story of their lives …

They still loved their mother-in-law, though.

Who wouldn't?

Chapter 24

December 18th

A bang echoed as Gio slammed the front door to their Amityville home. Happily, he shouted down the hall for his wife, knowing she was home. Her car had been outside, after all. He found Kim sitting on the couch in the living room.

Kim worked at the coffee table. Rolls of wrapping paper, tape, ribbons, fancy cards and bows sat all around in a scattered mess. She couldn't just wrap a gift and be done with it. That wouldn't be good enough for his wife. No, she had to do the whole ribbons, bows, and handmade cards thing.

It was a bit much for him.

But it made Kim happy.

A few wrapped gifts sat on the floor, finished and pretty. She was still working on quite a pile, though. Gifts for family and friends, likely. He knew she already had the majority of their gifts all wrapped.

Her head popped up as he shouted again.

"I did it! It's fucking done!"

Andino pushed up from the train tracks he was putting together on the floor at the sound of his father's shouts. "Papa's home!"

Kim gave her son a look, and shook her head. Unlike when *she* swore, Andino said nothing when his father did it. Giovanni had talked to the boy about being a tattletale, like Kim wanted him to. So now, the boy didn't tattle on his father. He couldn't help that Andino had not gotten the point that he was also not supposed to rat on everyone else, too.

One thing at a time …

Andino darted across the room, and ran full force into his father's legs. His arms wrapped tightly around Gio's body, and looked up with a wide smile.

"Hi, Dad."

Gio grinned back at his boy. "Hey, buddy."

"Will you play trains with me?"

"In a minute, I sure will."

Andino's smile grew impossibly wider. "Okay."

His son gave him one more hug, and then let go of his father to head back to the tracks and trains spread out on the floor.

Usually, Andino wasn't so clingy with his father, especially at his age. Gio figured it was because he had been gone so much lately, and when he was home, Andino felt the need to get all the attention and time he could out of his dad.

Gio didn't mind.

"What did you get done?" Kim asked.

She had gone back to her task of wrapping yet another Christmas gift. Some kind of luxury perfume set— probably for Catrina because that was exactly something his sister-in-law would like.

Gio dropped down on the couch with a heavy thud. Kim dropped the scissors and tape in her hands with a yelp as he wrapped his arms tightly around her waist, and pulled her into his lap. Laughing, she resituated herself to straddle his legs.

He kissed her once, then twice, and finally a third time.

Lingering …

Tasting …

Loving.

He deserved it, after everything.

"Gross," came a quiet voice a few feet away.

"Mind your business," Gio said over his wife's shoulder.

Andino made a gagging noise in the back of his throat.

Damn kid ...

Kim put her hands to Gio's cheeks, and turned him to face her. "Hey, look at me. What did you do that you feel the need to shout about it?"

"Lucian."

His wife stilled, and then a slow smile grew on her face. "Did you ...?"

"I did."

"Really?"

"Yep," Gio said. "Got the final details in today, and had a chat with the judge who is willing to sign off on everything, plus got the agreement done up with the D.A."

"Oh, my God, Gio!"

Kim kissed him that time—harder than he had kissed her. Happy, fast, and giggling all the while. It only added to the pride swelling in his chest. Going back to school to finish his law degree had paid off after all.

"Is he out already?"

"Tomorrow," Gio said. "But not one fucking word, Kim. Antony wants to surprise Jordyn and the kids, not to mention Ma. Lucian doesn't even know yet."

"Yeah, yeah. Hopes up, and all. I know. Still, this is going to be the *best* Christmas for those kids. They miss him so freaking much, it's crazy."

"You still can't say a word, Kim. It's done, though. Practically."

Kim let out her own shout of joy then, and kissed him again. She winked as she rested her forehead against his. "Knew you could do it, baby."

Gio chuckled. "There was never any doubt."

Okay, there was a *little* doubt.

Gio still handled his fucking business.

No matter what.

One more kiss from his wife …

One more gagging sound from the kid on the floor.

So was his life.

• • •

December 20th

Dante slid in beside Gio as Lucian and Jordyn danced in the middle of the great hall together. Gio would have

181

been dancing with his own wife, but Kim had taken Andino to go see the Santa Claus who had showed up for the kids.

"He looks happy," Dante said.

Gio passed his older brother a smile. "And so do you."

Dante nodded. "Apparently, I needed a break."

"Technically, you're still on it."

A hand clapped firmly to Gio's shoulder as Dante said, "Yes, and I have you to thank for that. Dad, too."

"I think I'll save your thanks for a later date when *I* need a break, Dante."

"Noted, man."

"Where's Cat?"

Dante laughed at the mention of his wife. "Making sure her orders are being followed to the letter in the kitchen."

"Ah."

"I'll probably go save the staff soon."

"It could be Ma," Gio pointed out.

"Truth. The mansion looks great."

Gio took in all the decorations. He liked the different color schemes in each room. All the guests were given something new to look at depending on where they partied. It was quite a sight. He now understood how hard his wife had truly worked with her sisters-in-law to get this whole thing done, not to mention *on* time, and to Cecelia's liking.

"Our wives can throw a damn good party," Gio said.

"That they can. You good?"

"Yeah."

Dante snuck a glass of champagne from a waiter as the man passed, and raised his brow at Gio. "Time to go save the poor fuckers in the kitchen from the wrath of Catrina Marcello."

Gio laughed, but honestly … Catrina could be a handful. Dante wasn't exactly overstating his wife's attitude. Not at all.

Once his brother was gone, Gio turned his attention to finding his own wife and son. Andino was just climbing down from the jolly Santa's lap when Gio stepped into the foyer. Antony made his way over as Andino chattered away to his mother about whales and Santa Claus.

"He's still going on about that, is he?" Antony asked.

Gio sighed. "Yep."

"Still haven't figured something out for him?"

"Nope. First time my son is going to be disappointed in me, I think."

"Santa, not you. Besides, another year and the whole Santa thing will be a far stretch for him, anyway."

"Point is, it still comes back to *me*."

Antony smiled a little. "Worry not, Gio. I am sure *something* will work out for Andino."

"Right."

His father lifted a finger and waved it. "Believe in Christmas magic, son. Believe."

Uh-huh.

"Why are you wearing a Santa hat?" Gio asked.

Antony gave him a look. "Don't talk or ask about that."

"Because Ma made you wear it?"

"I said don't talk or ask about it."

Because, yeah, Cecelia totally made Antony wear it.

Chapter 25

December 24th

Kim's body practically flew two inches up off the bed when Giovanni jumped on it. She shot him a fake glare that he entirely ignored as he buried his face into a pillow and groaned loudly.

"He's in bed, right?"

"Gruuumpff."

"What?"

More mumbles came from her husband.

With a laugh, Kim reached over and smacked Gio on his arm. "Stop it. Look at me so I can understand you, smartass."

Gio tipped his head to the side just enough for Kim to see half of his face as he said, "*Finally*, yes, he is in bed."

"Andino is excited, that's all."

"Oh, my God, Kim. It's fucking ten o'clock."

"And you stay up until one every morning. What's your point?"

"But not that long with him. Do you know how exhausting he is when he just goes, and goes, and fucking *goes*. He's like an energizer bunny but with speed. You know, the good kind—makes your heart race and your vision blur because everything is just so fast. Except with that kind of speed, you don't get out of breath like you do with him, and you don't get sore and tired until you crash."

"You haven't taken speed in like … ten years."

"Something like that," Gio mumbled. "Fact remains, that's what he's like, but I'm not young anymore and he tires me out."

Kim rolled her eyes. "You're fine."

"My legs hurt."

"You tired him out, likely."

"Probably," her husband agreed.

Then, Gio buried his face back into the pillow. Kim decided to let him stay like that for a little while if only because soon enough they would both have to get out of their comfy, warm bed. After all, Santa had to come for

Andino before morning.

That meant the two of them would spend a couple of hours downstairs setting extra gifts up, making everything look nice, and filling their son's stocking. Not to mention, eating the cookies, drinking the milk the boy left out … Gio could handle eating the carrot, though. Kim fucking hated carrots.

And marriage *was* about compromise, so …

A few minutes passed them by in silence before Gio turned to look at Kim once more. His green gaze drifted over her before he said quietly, "I still didn't find something for Andino that would satisfy the whales. A stuffed whale, and the documentary or whatever that he hasn't seen yet, but still, yeah."

Too little, too late.

It was Christmas Eve.

"It'll be fine, Gio," Kim assured.

It wasn't like Andino was spoiled, or anything. In fact, it was quite the opposite. Their son was kind of like a free range kid in the way they simply let him wander his interests from one thing or another. They didn't overwhelm him with stuff and *things*. If Andino showed interest in something particular, then they helped to feed into that interest, but nothing more.

The whales were the same thing.

Eventually, he would move on to something else.

"He really didn't ask for much, Kim," Gio pointed out. "A couple of things, something for someone else, and a fucking *whale*."

Kim laughed softly. "Exactly. Our son—who's *six*, by the way—thought to write on his Santa list for someone else, Gio. He barely thought about things he wanted, and those things were basically immaterial. He put something for John closer to the top, like it was a big priority. And the whale thing? At the very bottom, like an afterthought."

"Yeah, but—"

"You said it, Gio. He's not stupid. He's little. He's young. His attention bounces back and forth at times, but he's *not* stupid. What he really wanted, he got. Don't fret."

"Shouldn't that just make me feel like an even bigger piece of shit, then?"

Kim frowned. "What, why?"

"Because he's that good of a damn kid. Because he's tenderhearted, or something. I don't know. Because he asked for Santa to bring John's dad home, but he won't even get what he wanted the most."

"You're overthinking this, Gio."

"No, I think it makes perfect—"

The ring of a doorbell stopped her husband from saying anything else. They had the doorbell speakers wired all throughout their home so that no matter where they were, they would hear it.

Kim pushed out of the bed first, but Gio followed right after.

"Me first," he told her. "Who the fuck is ringing our bell at ten at night on Christmas Eve? I don't like that at all."

"Stop being paranoid, Gio. It's Christmas."

"Hush, woman."

Kim glowered at his back, but decided not to say more. It wasn't long before they were downstairs, and whoever it was waiting outside rang the doorbell twice more in quick succession.

"Well, whoever it is, they're persistent."

"Persistent about getting my fist through their face if they wake up my kid," Gio muttered.

"Stop being nasty, it's—"

"Christmas. Yeah, yeah." Gio yanked opened the front door with a harsh, "What?"

On the other side of the door standing on their front stoop was a man Kim recognized, but couldn't bring forth his name. He was young—maybe twenty-two or so, if that. An enforcer for the Marcello family who often watched over the Marcello home or took Cecelia places when she wasn't in the mood to drive.

"Nate," Gio said, "what are you doing here?"

The young man wore a Santa cap on his head, and held out a small white gift box with a perfect red bow on top. The box was maybe a foot-long by six-inches wide.

"Someone wanted this sent along, Skip."

Gio took the box, and eyed it. "Someone like my mother or father?"

"Or Santa?" Nate smiled. "Not supposed to say, you know."

"All right. Thanks, man."

Nate gave a two finger salute, and headed back down the steps without as much as a look over his shoulder. Gio closed the door once the man was out of sight, and then turned to face his wife with the gift in his hands.

"Are you going to open it or not?" Kim asked.

"Should probably wait for morning, shouldn't—"

Screw that.

Kim snagged the box from Gio's hand, and popped the top off. Inside, plane tickets and papers with information on a whale watching tour rested on top of white tissue paper. On top of those sat a handwritten note.

To Gio and Andino, it read. *Santa thought a whale watching trip in Vancouver, Canada might be a little bit better than an actual whale inside your house.*

—Love Santa

"Oh, wow," Kim said, unable to form much else for words.

Gio picked out the note, and read it over a good ten times before a smile lifted the edges of his mouth into a full blown grin. "You know …"

"That's totally your dad's handwriting."

"Yeah," Gio said.

"Merry Christmas, Gio."

Gio laughed as he tapped the note against his palm. Then, he kissed his wife. "Merry Christmas, Kim. Ready to set some shit up?"

"You say that like we have a choice."

He looked down at the note again. "Not really concerned about tomorrow, now. Looking forward to it, actually."

She bet.

Antony & Cecelia

December 25th

Antony didn't mind the Santa hat as much, now.

He felt as though he might deserve to wear it, after all.

The very large, and *very* loud Marcello clan gathered in the living room, each brother tucked into a seating place with their wife and kids.

Lucian—having gotten permission to spend Christmas at his parents' home despite house arrest—sat with Jordyn and their three little ones closest to the large Christmas tree. His oldest son managed to give his wife

192

attention while he deflected Cella's effort to open the first gift Antony had passed to her.

Giovanni, his youngest, had Kim sitting in his lap while Andino read through a facts book about killer whales. For the *fifth* time.

Dante, sitting near the fireplace with Catrina and their two kids, finally looked relaxed for the first time in what seemed like months. His son and daughter were both tucked in close to their father's side while Catrina sat higher on a chaise behind them, and leaned down to chat.

"Are we ready to start?" Cecelia asked.

Then, his wife spied the gift Cella already had in her hands. She turned to Antony with a raised eyebrow.

He only shrugged.

"You started playing Santa already," she accused.

Didn't she know?

He had been playing Santa for weeks now.

She had wanted one thing for Christmas, and that was all her kids together, under their roof to celebrate the holidays.

It hadn't been easy.

Antony pulled a lot of strings.

So worth it.

"Well, get under the tree Antony and find a gift for everybody," his wife ordered.

193

Antony didn't need to be told a second time. Cecelia spoke, and he listened. He had learned over the years that was the best way for them to be. He didn't mind at all.

It didn't take long for Antony to paw through the piles of Christmas gifts, and find one for each person. They had quite a few to get through, but that was okay, too. They had all the time in the world now that Mass was over, and lunch had been served.

Once everyone had a gift in their hands—minus Antony and Cecelia—the tearing of wrapping paper started. Antony and Cecelia would wait for later, once they were alone, to open their gifts.

Antony tucked his wife in tight to his side, and kissed her temple.

Cecelia smiled softly up at him.

"You didn't think the yacht and island were your only gifts, did you?" he asked.

"I could have asked for the moon and stars, Antony."

"I would have given those to you, too, Cecelia."

"Of course you would have."

"The island trip *was* a real thing," Antony said, chuckling. "If all else failed, I was going to take you to the island and distract you for a couple of weeks."

"We can do that after the holidays."

Most definitely.

Close to the top of their ten foot high tree, a single extra-large glass ornament glinted under the white twinkle lights. Out of all the Christmas decorations in their home, that one was Antony's favorite.

It was clear, with white and silver snowflakes inside. Twice the size of a baseball, it always had to be hung on a strong branch. He was the one to hang it every year just to be safe. His wife had given it to them on their very first Christmas together after they married.

A simple ornament that meant the world to him. It only had a single line of scripted words written across the middle.

But back then, when Cecelia had given it to him, he read the one line and knew someday it wouldn't be just them opening gifts on Christmas morning. It wouldn't forever be a family of two like they had been that first Christmas.

He still stopped to read the words on that ornament every single Christmas after the first one. It still meant the world, even when his whole world was already sitting in his living room, and tucked into his side.

Merry Christmas from the Marcellos.

Cross + Catherine

Always
Revere
Unruly

Guzzi Duet

Unraveled, Book One
Entangled, Book Two

DeLuca Duet

Waste of Worth: Part One
Worth of Waste: Part Two

Standalone Titles

Inflict

Donati Bloodlines

Thin Lies
Thin Lines
Thin Lives
Behind the Bloodlines
The Complete Trilogy

Filthy Marcellos

Antony
Lucian
Giovanni
Dante
Legacy
A Very Marcello Christmas
The Complete Collection

Seasons of Betrayal

Where the Sun Hides
Where the Snow Falls
Where the Wind Whispers

Gun Moll Trilogy

Gun Moll
Gangster Moll
Madame Moll

The Chicago War

Deathless & Divided
Reckless & Ruined

Scarless & Sacred
Breathless & Bloodstained
The Complete Series

The Russian Guns

The Arrangement
The Life
The Score
Demyan & Ana
Shattered
The Jersey Vignettes

Find more on Bethany-Kris's website at

www.bethanykris.com.

For those who may not know, as I did only say it once on my Facebook page, this Christmas novella will be the final book I write for the original first generation of Marcellos. It's a bittersweet thing—I love them so much, and could write them into forever. Hell, I'm already into their kids, and even the grandkids are in there, too.

So yeah, this is sad for me to say goodbye officially. But these books would not have been what they were without the readers and fans of these Filthy men and their wives. Thank you so much for loving them like you did. It was this series where I finally started to think, *Damn, maybe I've got something here*. Because of all of you, truly.

To Tracy, thank you for proofing. And to Eli, for editing,

and working your magic like you do.

Sasha, thank you for the teasers and the cover—they're all amazing, just like you, love.

Hugs, loves.

Bethany-Kris

Bethany-Kris is a Canadian author, lover of much, and mother to four young sons, one cat, and three dogs. A small town in Eastern Canada where she was born and raised is where she has always called home. With her boys under her feet, a snuggling cat, barking dogs, and a spouse calling over his shoulder, she is nearly always writing something ... when she can find the time.

Find Bethany-Kris at:
Her website www.bethanykris.com or on Facebook at www.facebook.com/bethanykriswrites on her blog at http://www.bethanykris.com/blog or on Twitter - @BethanyKris.

Sign up to Bethany-Kris's New Release Newsletter here: http://eepurl.com/bf9lzD.